Veil of Echoes

Zora Stone

Print ISBN: 978-1-971405-07-0

Publisher: Smut by Design

www.zorastone.com

Broken mirrors reflect the most light.
(And make more rainbows, just sayin'.)

PREVIOUSLY IN THE ETHER CHRONICLES

A quick refresher before we dive into mirrors and madness

Hey there, lovely readers! Ready to step through the looking glass? Here's what you need to remember before things get properly complicated:

Crown of the Mist:

Bree survived alone with silver mist as her only companion until her five childhood friends finally stopped pining from a distance. Her creepy landlord Phil got handsy, Bree's power exploded (very satisfying), she touched a mysterious crown, and boom—she's the last Source, magic is real, and apparently she's kind of a big deal.

Into the Ether:

Enter Thane—gorgeous, dangerous, deadly, and a vampire-class Feeder sent by the Council to investigate. He arrived planning to control Bree but got distracted when she accidentally rebuilt an entire magical sanctuary. The place literally reshaped itself around her. Magical refugees showed up. Stellan appeared to provide sarcastic commentary and suspiciously helpful information. The guys all developed their own powers, glowed slightly, and looked unfairly attractive while doing it.

Ashen Oath:

Things got real. Bree discovered the ancient Mirror Rite chamber beneath the sanctuary—a place where magical beings once merged with their mirror selves to become whole. Except Bree's mirror self? That's Riley. Confident, certain, regal Riley—everything Bree fears becoming.

Then Phil attacked. And Seth—sweet, helpful Seth who'd been quietly walking the gardens—betrayed her. In her rage and devastation, Bree's Ether exploded out of control and Seth turned to ash right in front of them. She killed him. The group was shattered. Bree was destroyed by what she'd done.

When the dust settled, Bree went into the chamber alone. No one knows what happened inside—she won't talk about it. But when she emerged, the mirrors were no longer broken. The Ashen Oath chamber had changed.

And so had Bree.

Welcome to Veil of Echoes.

Hope you're ready for mirrors that remember, secrets that won't stay buried, and the unsettling feeling that not everything—or everyone—has come back the same.

(Fair warning: reflections can lie.)

Trigger Warnings

Thank you for reading *Veil of Echoes*. This book contains themes and content that may be triggering to some readers. Please review the following warnings before proceeding:

Emotional & Psychological Themes

- **Captivity & Imprisonment** – Prolonged isolation in supernatural realm, loss of agency

- **Psychological Manipulation & Gaslighting** – Sustained emotional control, reality distortion, coercion

- **Identity Theft & Replacement** – Being replaced by another; watching someone wear your life

- **Corruption & Mental Influence** – Magical manipulation of thoughts, desires, and sense of self

- **PTSD & Trauma Responses** – Panic attacks, dissociation, traumatic memory triggers

- **Betrayal & Deception** – Major revelations about trusted individuals; questioning reality

- **Suicidal Ideation & Hopelessness** – Characters experiencing despair in dire circumstances

- **Emotional Abuse** – Grooming, isolation tactics, weaponized affection

Violence & Supernatural Threats

- **Supernatural Horror** – Void realm, otherworldly predators, existential terror

- **Physical Restraint & Captivity** – Being held against will, magical bindings

- **Blood & Feeding** – Vampire feeding, magical consumption, life-force drain

- **Stalking & Pursuit** – Being hunted across supernatural realms

- **Physical Confrontations** – Magical combat, violence, injury

Intimacy & Relationships

- **Explicit Sexual Content** – Detailed intimate scenes between adults (multiple instances)

- **Dubious Consent** – Sexual encounters under magical influence/corruption

- **Polyamorous Dynamics** – Multiple simultaneous romantic/sexual relationships

- **Magical Bonding** – Soul-deep connections with permanent, life-altering consequences

- **Intimacy Under Duress** – Sexual/romantic encounters in captivity situations

- **Relationship Manipulation** – Using intimacy as control mechanism

Dark Magic & Supernatural Elements

- **Magical Corruption** – Power being actively tainted; loss of self to dark influence

- **Reality Distortion** – Mirror realms, doppelgängers, questioning what's real

- **Possession/Body Theft** – Characters being replaced or controlled by external forces

- **Void/Dark Realm** – Otherworldly dimension, existential isolation, time distortion

- **Predatory Supernatural Beings** – Entities that feed on life force, emotions, or souls

- **Forced Transformation** – Magical changes imposed without full consent

Family & Authority

- **Past Abuse References** – Ongoing impact of childhood trauma

- **Power Imbalances** – Political manipulation, magical hierarchy, systemic oppression

- **Governmental Persecution** – Council surveillance, threats of magical binding/stripping

- **Discrimination** – Prejudice against specific magical classes (Feeders)

This list is provided to ensure a safe reading experience. If any of these topics are personally distressing, please read with care and compassion for yourself.

Thank you for continuing this journey with Bree and her chosen family.

Zora Stone

CONTENTS

Part One: The Beautiful Lie

Chapter 1
RHETT

Heat jolts awake under my skin before my brain catches up.

I open my eyes to see the sanctuary's runes falter—warmth ripped from the walls like someone snuffed out an ancient candle. My fire magic surges in response, wild and restless, and I'm fully awake in seconds.

The bed beside me is empty.

The sheets are cooling too fast, warmth being pulled from them by something unseen. No lingering scent on the pillow, no trace of how she'd curled against me after we'd finally collapsed into sleep, exhausted from everything that happened with the Oath.

She was here. She was definitely here when I fell asleep.

Now there's nothing.

I sit up, heart hammering. "Bree?"

My voice echoes strangely in her circular bedroom, like the space is bigger than it should be. The horned mirror she found weeks ago sits untouched on her dresser, only reflecting my panic. The reading nook where Theo usually plants himself is empty.

Even the air feels wrong—too still, too quiet.

"Bree!" I call louder, already throwing myself out of bed.

Nothing.

I grab jeans from the floor, pulling them on as I stride toward the door. The sanctuary's wrongness crawls up my spine like a warning. My hands are already warm, fire magic responding to my panic.

The common area is empty when I burst through her door. All the connecting bedroom doors are closed, the silence too thick.

"Bree!" The shout tears out before I can think.

I tear through their rooms—Wes tangled in sheets, jolting awake; Jace cursing as he rolls upright from sleeping upside down; Theo blinking groggily in his doorway; Gray standing next to his bed like he never even tried to sleep. Not one of them with Bree.

"What's happening?" Wes asks, voice rough.

"Bree's missing," Theo says, and something in his tone makes everyone pause.

"Missing how?" Jace demands.

"I don't know!" I'm pacing now, heat radiating from my skin. "She was there when I fell asleep, and now she's just—gone. No note, no trace, nothing."

"The sanctuary," Wes says suddenly. "It doesn't feel right."

He feels it too. The warm pulse of protection that's become as familiar as breathing is flickering like a dying flame.

We spread out through the common area, but before any of us can suggest where to search, voices drift from the main hallway. Low, urgent conversation.

I storm toward the sound, the others following behind me.

Thane and Stellan stand near the large windows overlooking the grounds, both fully dressed despite the early hour. They're talking in the kind of hushed tones that mean trouble, heads bent close together.

They look up when we appear—a pack of half-dressed, panicked men led by me in nothing but jeans and barely contained fire.

"She's not fucking here!" I announce before either of them can speak.

Thane goes completely still. "What do you mean she's not here?"

"I mean she's gone! Vanished! I've checked every room—"

"Where could she have gone?" Gray asks quietly.

"The chamber," Stellan breathes, cutting me off.

Something that feels a lot like dread creeps up my spine.

"No," Jace says immediately, taking a step back. "She wouldn't. Not alone. Not without—"

"She would," Thane says grimly. "If she thought it was her choice to make."

Stellan is already moving toward the corridor that leads deeper into the sanctuary. "She shouldn't do it alone. If she's taking the Oath, we have to stop her."

We follow him toward the back door that leads out to the garden—the path that winds deeper into the sanctuary grounds, toward the chamber. We move like a pack of wolves chasing the scent of our missing heart. Behind me, Theo's breathing changes like he's trying to force a vision. Wes's footsteps falter once, his hunger clearly gnawing at him. Jace's knives appear in his hands without him seeming to think about it. Gray and Thane walk behind us, watching for threats just in case.

The journey to the Chamber seems longer than it was yesterday, the shadows deeper. Almost like the Sanctuary grounds are trying to prevent us from getting there.

When we finally reach the chamber entrance, the door stands open.

Silver light spills out from within, brighter than it's ever been. But there's something else threading through it now—something darker that makes my fire magic recoil.

"Bree," I whisper.

We descend the stairs in single file, and I can feel the exact moment each of them sees her.

She stands before the largest mirror in the center ring, one hand pressed flat against the glass. Light radiates from the point of contact. Silver shot through with black, like ink bleeding through water. The kind we've become accustomed to since Bree's visit to the Void.

As we watch her Ether swirls around her feet, and it becomes completely inverted—black mist threaded with silver. It moves differently too, more controlled, more purposeful.

I pull my focus away from the unsettling Ether and focus on Bree. She looks different. She still looks like the Bree I know, but there's something about the way she holds herself. Straighter. More certain. Like someone who's never doubted her place in the world.

"Bree," I call out, but she doesn't turn.

Her reflection in the mirror flinches at something unseen just for a moment, but when I blink, it's gone.

Stellan makes a sound behind me—low, sharp, like recognition he doesn't want to name.

"What?" I demand, but he's already moving down the remaining stairs.

"Bree," Thane calls, his voice carrying command I've never heard before. "Step away from the mirror. Now."

That gets her attention. She turns, and when her eyes meet mine, something in my chest feels uneasy.

They're still green, still beautiful, but they hold confidence I've never seen before, never thought I'd see on Bree.

"You came," she says, and her voice sounds pleased rather than defensive. "Good. You should see this."

"See what?" Gray asks quietly. He's appeared beside me without my noticing, fully dressed and alert.

She turns back to the mirror, pressing both hands against the glass now. The light flares brighter, and her reflection moves completely out of sync with her actual movements.

"The completion," she says simply. "The choice I was always meant to make."

Flames dance under my skin, wild and restless. She stands in front of the mirror like she's finally found calm, and it terrifies me.

The black Ether around her feet pulses once, like a heartbeat, and every instinct I have screams that something isn't right.

The woman touching the mirror might look like Bree, might sound like Bree.

But she's not afraid.

And Bree is always afraid, just a little. It's part of who she is—the careful way she moves through the world, the defensive curl to her shoulders, the way she checks over her shoulder for threats that might be following.

This woman has none of that.

This woman looks like she's never been broken at all.

"Bree," I say carefully, "what happened to you?"

She glances back at me, and for just a moment, something vulnerable flickers in her expression. Like she's afraid I won't like what I see.

But then it's gone, replaced by that unfamiliar certainty.

"I became who I was always meant to be," she says.

The mirror pulses with dark light, and I realize with growing horror that we might be too late to stop whatever's happening.

But looking at her now—confident, transformed, finally unafraid—I can't tell if we've lost her to something terrible, or if she's right and she's finally found who she was always meant to be.

Chapter 2
JACE

"And she is magnificent," I say, clapping my hands together with a grin.

Look at her. Actually look. The way she holds herself—straight-backed, chin up, like she finally knows she belongs in her own skin. No hunched shoulders, no defensive curl, no checking over her shoulder for threats that might be following. She's standing there like she owns the space instead of apologizing for taking it up.

This is what I've been waiting for. What we've all been waiting for.

While the others stand frozen in whatever horror-spiral they're having, I step forward. Because that's what you do when someone you love finally stops being afraid—you don't question it, you celebrate it.

"Come on," I say, wrapping my arm around her shoulders and guiding her away from the mirror. "Let's get you out of here."

She leans into me without hesitation, and something in my chest unclenches. This is what I've wanted for her since the day we met—to trust without flinching, to accept comfort without calculating the cost.

Though there's something different about her scent. Sharper. Like ozone before a storm.

I push the thought aside as we head toward the chamber stairs. Behind us, the others follow in a silence so thick I could cut it with one of my blades.

"What the hell just happened back there?" I ask quietly as we climb.

"I'm not sure." Her voice is steady, certain in a way that makes me want to grin. "Words just... came to me. I spoke them. But nothing really happened."

"You're still here," I tell her, meaning it. "That's all that matters."

She smiles, and it reaches her eyes—something that looks like relief flooding her expression. Like she was afraid I might not accept this version of her, and I just proved her wrong.

We emerge from the chamber into the pre-dawn air, and I can feel the others' tension radiating behind us like heat from a forge. Rhett's practically vibrating with whatever internal fire he's fighting. Theo keeps shooting glances at Bree like he's trying to force a vision. Wes looks pale and distracted, probably fighting hunger. And Gray...

Gray's silent in that way that means he's cataloging every detail and finding them all wrong.

They just don't see it yet. She's stronger. This is *good*.

"Maybe I just needed to finally stop being afraid," she says, and there's something almost teasing in her tone that makes my heart skip.

Bree never teased. Not like that. Not with that underlying confidence that suggests she knows exactly what effect her words have.

But maybe that's just who she was always meant to be.

"About time," I say, squeezing her shoulder. "We've been waiting for you to realize you're a badass."

She laughs, and the sound is lighter than I've ever heard from her. Like she's finally breathing freely after holding her breath for years.

The sanctuary's runes flicker as we approach the main building, the protective wards seeming uncertain. But Bree doesn't even notice, just stretches like she's coming home after a long journey.

In the common area, she settles onto the couch with easy grace while the rest of us hover around like we're not sure what to do with this new reality.

"So," I say, breaking the silence because someone has to. "She came back to us. That's all we need to know."

"Back from where?" Theo asks quietly. "Rhett said she was gone, but she was just in the chamber."

"I was always in the chamber," Bree says simply. "I just... found myself there."

The explanation should feel inadequate. Should raise more questions than it answers. But looking at her—really looking—I see someone who's finally comfortable in her own skin. Someone who's stopped apologizing for taking up space.

Even if she feels a little different, isn't this what we all wanted? Bree, but stronger? Bree, but unafraid?

"The important thing is that you're safe," I say firmly, catching each of their gazes in turn. "Whatever happened in that chamber, she came through it. She came through it better."

Rhett's jaw ticks, but he doesn't argue. Gray's still watching her with those calculating eyes. Wes just looks relieved that she's here, whatever version of here this is.

"I'm tired," she says, standing smoothly. "It's been a long night."

"Do you want company?" The offer slips out before I can think about it, and I realize I mean it. Not in any way that would pressure her, just... I don't want her to be alone. Not after everything.

She considers this with a tilt of her head that's somehow both familiar and foreign. "Actually, yes. I think I'd like that."

The others exchange glances that I pretend not to see. Let them have their doubts. Let them overthink every word and gesture.

All I know is that for the first time since I've known her, Bree Holloway looks at me without a trace of fear. Without walls or barriers or the careful distance she's always maintained.

And I'll fight anyone who tries to take that away from her.

"Lead the way," I tell her, ignoring the weight of the others' stares.

Because sometimes, when someone you love finally finds their strength, you don't question the gift. You just hold onto it and refuse to let go.

Chapter 3
THANE

I watch them disappear down the hallway toward her bedroom—Jace's arm wrapped around her shoulders like she's something precious he's afraid of losing. His voice carries back to us, bright with relief and determination to celebrate whatever just happened.

The rest of us remain in the common room, none of us quite ready to disperse.

Because we all felt it. The wrongness that clings to the air like smoke.

I've lived long enough to recognize the scent of power unleashed without understanding. The electric charge that comes when ancient things wake up and start paying attention. Whatever happened in that chamber, it wasn't the simple ritual Jace wants to believe it was.

"Anyone else notice her Ether looked different?" I ask, finally giving voice to what we're all thinking.

The question hangs between us for a moment before Rhett nods grimly. "Black with silver running through it."

"I saw it too," Gray says quietly, his sharp eyes still fixed on the path they took. There's something conflicted in his expression, like he's fighting between relief and unease.

I study each of their faces in turn. Rhett's jaw is tight with the kind of frustrated protectiveness that usually leads to him punching something.

Wes looks pale, one hand pressed to his stomach—the hunger is clearly gnawing at him, but there's something else there too. Fear, maybe. Or recognition.

And Gray... Gray's watching the space where she stood like he's trying to decide if he's seeing a ghost.

Wes shifts beside me. "But she's okay, right? She *has* to be okay."

Rhett growls, "She didn't look okay."

The words carry more weight than he probably intended. Because he's right. She looked confident, yes. Stronger. But there was something underneath that strength that felt borrowed rather than earned.

"What do you mean?" Wes asks, and the desperation in his voice makes something twist in my chest.

"Something's off," Rhett says bluntly. "The way she moved. Talked. All of it."

Stellan's gray eyes are unreadable in the pre-dawn light. "I don't know," he says finally. "But something happened in the chamber."

"Do you think she took the Oath?" Rhett presses.

"I'm not sure." Stellan's voice carries that careful precision he uses when he's weighing his words. "But the chamber felt alive this time. More alive than it did yesterday."

That sends a chill through me. I've felt ancient magic before—the kind that pulses with its own hunger, its own agenda. The kind that makes bargains in languages older than memory and always collects what it's owed.

If the chamber is waking up, if it's responding to whatever Bree did...

"The chamber," I say suddenly. "Did anyone notice how different it looked?"

"What do you mean?" Gray asks.

"All the mirrors were intact. Perfect. And the ash..." I pause, letting the implication hang. "The ash piles were gone."

The silence that follows is heavy with implications none of us want to examine too closely. Because yesterday, that chamber was a graveyard. This morning, it looked like it had been waiting for her.

Stellan goes still—too still. "I saw it," he says, and nothing else, though it looks like he wants to.

"She's here," Gray says, but his tone lacks conviction. "That's what matters."

"Is it?" The words slip out before I can stop them.

Gray's attention snaps to me, sharp and dangerous. "What's that supposed to mean?"

I choose my words carefully. "I'm saying maybe we should be asking who came back from that chamber, not just celebrating that someone did."

"That's Bree," Wes says fiercely. "You saw her. You heard her voice."

"Did I?" I let the question hang in the air. "Or did I hear someone using her voice?"

Rhett takes a step toward me, heat radiating from his skin. "What the hell are you implying?"

"I'm implying that ancient magic doesn't work without consequence. And if that's what she did—if she attempted an Oath like that—something else might have answered instead of the chamber accepting her."

The words are harsher than I intended, but they needed to be said. Someone has to be willing to voice the doubts we're all carrying.

"You think someone else is wearing her face?" Gray asks quietly.

"I think we should be prepared for possibilities beyond 'she's finally healed,'" I reply. "Because if there's one thing I've learned about magic this old, it's that it always has teeth."

Wes wraps his arms around himself. "But the way she looked at Jace. That was real."

"Emotions can be mimicked," I point out. "And the way someone looks at you depends entirely on who's doing the looking."

Theo staggers suddenly, one hand flying to his temple. We all turn toward him instinctively, but he waves us off even as his eyes lose focus.

"What do you see?" Wes asks, voice tight with worry.

"Chains. Silver chains. She's kneeling, surrendering to something... someone. Heavy. Tangible. Real."

"Stop," Rhett snaps, fire flickering under his skin. "Just stop talking."

But the image has already taken root. Chains. Surrender. Not the triumphant transformation Jace wants to believe in, but something else entirely.

Something that sounds disturbingly like captivity.

"Darkness," he breathes. "But not empty darkness. Hungry darkness. And she's..." He stops, blinking hard as the vision releases him. "She's choosing it."

Something cold settles in my stomach. We stand in the growing dawn light, each of us wrestling with what that might mean.

I think of the Void. Of Bree's face when we were trapped there together, the way her expression changed when she heard something I couldn't. The look in her eyes—not fear, but recognition. Like she was listening to a voice that knew her name.

She never told me what she heard in that darkness. But I remember the way she went still, the way her breathing changed—deeper, like when we were together. The way she looked like she was considering something I couldn't see. Chains. Surrender. Choosing darkness.

Maybe Theo's visions aren't as symbolic as we want to believe.

"Theo." I keep my voice level, unthreatening. "What else do you see?"

He shakes his head, pressing the heel of his hand against his forehead. "It's fading. But there was... water? No, not water. Something that moved like water but felt cold. Dead."

I lock eyes with Stellan. "The Void," I say quietly.

Stellan gives the barest nod, and I know he understands.

Everyone else turns to look at me, and I realize I've said too much. But it's too late to take it back now.

"You think she's connected to the Void somehow?" Gray asks.

"I think she's been connected to it for longer than any of us realized." I run a hand through my hair, weighing how much to reveal. "When we were there together, she heard something. Something I couldn't. And whatever it was, it knew her."

"What kind of something?" Rhett demands.

"The kind that makes offers you never quite understand," I say simply. "The kind that promises everything you've ever wanted in exchange for something you don't think you'll miss."

The group falls into uneasy silence, each of us lost in our own thoughts. In the distance, I can still see the faint outline of Jace and Bree—or whoever she is now—disappearing into the sanctuary.

"If that's not really her," Wes says quietly, "then where is she?"

It's the question none of us want to ask, because the answers that come to mind are all variations on the same theme: trapped, lost, or worse.

"I don't know," I admit. "But if something did take her place, then the real Bree is somewhere we can't reach her. Somewhere we can't help."

"Unless we figure out what happened," Gray says.

"Unless we figure out what happened," I agree.

Rhett's hands clench into fists. "So what do we do?"

"We watch," I say. "We listen. We pay attention to every detail that doesn't quite fit. And we hope that whoever's wearing her face makes a mistake before it's too late to matter."

"And if she doesn't make mistakes?" Wes asks.

I look back at the chamber door, still feeling that pulse of wrongness seeping through the cracks. Still tasting the electric charge in the air that speaks of power unleashed and balances shifted.

"Then we learn to live with the consequences of getting exactly what we asked for."

Because they wanted Bree stronger. More certain. More willing to claim what she deserves.

Maybe they got exactly what they asked for.

But sometimes, when you get what you want, you discover it was never yours to begin with.

Chapter 4
WES

I can't breathe in there anymore.

The common room feels too small, too full of doubt and suspicion that tastes like copper on my tongue. My hands shake as I push through the back door into the garden, desperate for air that doesn't carry the weight of Thane's accusations.

It's Bree. It has to be Bree.

The hunger claws at my stomach, worse than it's been in weeks, but that's not what's making me sick. It's the way everyone looked at each other back there. The way Stellan went silent and Rhett's fire started building under his skin.

Like they're already planning for war.

I press the heels of my hands against my eyes, trying to stop the spiral before it takes me under completely. The garden feels different out here—lighter somehow, like it remembers what peace feels like even if I don't.

"It's her," I whisper to the empty air. "I'd know if it wasn't her. Wouldn't I?"

"Would you?"

I spin around to find Gray standing in the doorway, still as stone except for his eyes. They're too bright, too focused, scanning the garden like he's cataloging every shadow for threats.

"Don't," I say, backing up a step. "Don't you start doubting too."

Gray steps into the garden, closing the door behind him with deliberate care. He crosses to me in three quick strides, and before I can say anything else, his hands frame my face and he kisses me.

It starts gentle—his lips soft against mine, thumb brushing across my cheekbone like he's trying to memorize the feeling. But there's something desperate underneath, the way his mouth moves like he's trying to convince both of us that everything's still okay. When he deepens the kiss, I taste the fear he's trying so hard to hide.

When he pulls back, he wraps his arms around me, holding me against his chest with more force than necessary.

"I'm not doubting," he says quietly, but his voice is tight. "I'm trying to think."

I should feel better in his arms. Usually Gray's solid presence calms me. But right now his muscles are coiled like he's ready to spring into action at any second, and his heartbeat is too fast against my ear.

"About what?" I ask, pulling back to look at his face. "About whether the woman we've all been in love with for months is suddenly someone else? About whether we're all losing our minds?"

"About whether I failed her."

The words knock the air from my lungs. "What are you talking about?"

Gray steps away from me and moves further into the garden, his movements too controlled, like he's fighting something underneath his skin. "I should have stopped it. Then it never would have been able to take hold."

"Take hold of what?"

"Whoever's wearing her face now."

I flinch. "That's still Bree."

"I'm not sure it is," Gray's voice is quiet, deadly. "Because when she looked at me back there, for just a second, I thought it wasn't her at all."

The admission hangs between creating distance I don't want. Because Gray doesn't make mistakes about people. Gray sees everything, notices everything, remembers everything. If he's questioning what he saw...

"No." I shake my head, backing up until my shoulders hit the garden wall. "You're wrong. You have to be wrong."

"I hope I am." Gray's hands clench into fists at his sides. "But hoping doesn't make it true."

I watch him pace along the garden path, and something cold settles in my chest. Gray doesn't pace. Gray stands still and observes and makes calculated decisions. This restless energy radiating from him feels wrong.

"You've always protected her," I say, trying to find solid ground. "You're the one who kept us all together when everything went to hell."

"I fell asleep." His voice is flat, self-recriminating. "I should have stayed awake. Should have known she might go back to that chamber."

"We all fell asleep."

"I don't." Gray's hands clench into fists at his sides. "I never sleep through the night. I keep watch. That's what I do. But last night I was so exhausted I didn't even hear her leave."

The air around him shifts—subtle at first, then more noticeable. Like a pressure change before a storm, but concentrated entirely around Gray's body.

"What's happening?" I ask, because something is definitely happening.

Gray looks down at his hands like they belong to someone else. "I don't know."

But I do. Or at least, I think I do. The same way I can sense emotional hunger in a room, I can feel whatever's building in Gray. It's wild and desperate and completely at odds with his usual control.

"You need to calm down," I say carefully.

"Calm down?" Gray's voice cracks. "Bree is missing—or replaced, or corrupted, or dead—and you want me to calm down?"

"Gray—"

"I can't protect her if she's not really her!" The words explode out of him, and with them comes a pressure that makes my ears pop. "I can't save someone who doesn't exist!"

The air in the garden goes completely still. Even the leaves stop rustling.

I take a step toward him, hands raised like I'm approaching a spooked animal. "Hey. Look at me."

Gray's breathing is ragged, too fast, and there's something wrong with his eyes. They're shifting between gray and something else—something darker, more primal.

"I failed her," he whispers. "Whatever that thing is wearing her face, it's there because I wasn't strong enough to keep her safe."

"That's not true."

"Isn't it?" Gray's fists clench tighter. "She needed someone who would fight for her without hesitation. Someone who would burn the world down to keep her safe. Instead, she got *me*."

"She got someone who loves her."

"Love isn't enough." The words come out broken, desperate. "Love doesn't keep people from disappearing into chambers full of ash and mirrors."

Something in his voice makes me step closer despite every instinct screaming at me to give him space. "Gray, you're scaring me."

He looks up at me then, and for a moment I see past the control and the careful observation to the raw terror underneath. "Good. Because I'm scaring myself."

The pressure in the air builds again, and I realize what I'm seeing. Gray isn't just having a breakdown.

He's on the edge of something bigger. Something that might change him permanently.

"Whatever's happening," I say quietly, "we'll figure it out. Together. Don't leave me here thinking I'm the only one losing my mind."

Gray stares at me for a long moment, and I can see him fighting something internal. Like there are two different versions of him warring for control.

"It's Bree," I say again, because I have to believe it. "It has to be Bree. Because if it's not..."

I can't finish the sentence. Can't voice the fear that's been eating at me since the moment she looked at Jace with that confident smile.

Because if it's not Bree, then everything I thought I knew about connection and recognition and the way souls call to each other is wrong.

And I don't know how to keep going in a world where I can't trust my own heart to know the difference between truth and lie.

Gray doesn't answer. He just looks out at the garden like it's a battlefield only he can see, his hands still clenched, the air around him still humming with something that feels dangerous and wild and completely unlike the Gray I know.

And for the first time since this whole nightmare started, I wonder if we're all about to lose more than just Bree.

I wonder if we're about to lose ourselves too.

Chapter 5
GRAY

The bones in my spine feel like they're grinding against each other.

It starts there, between my shoulder blades, then spreads down through my ribs like fire. My skin is too tight, stretched over a frame that's trying to become something else entirely. Every breath feels like I'm drowning in my own body.

"Gray?" Wes's voice sounds far away even though he's right next to me. "What's wrong?"

I can't answer. Can't form words around the pressure building in my head, behind my eyes, in the space where my jaw connects to my skull. Something is clawing its way out from the inside, and I've been fighting it for so long I don't remember what it feels like to not be at war with myself.

Not now. Not in front of Wes.

But my body doesn't care what I want. The change has been building since Bree touched the crown—every time I felt the urge to pace, every moment of restless energy, every night I couldn't sleep because something under my skin was trying to break free. Her awakening triggered something in all of us, but I've held it back through sheer will. Bree's disappearance, the chamber, the growing certainty that I failed to protect her—it's all too much.

My knees buckle, and I hit the garden path hard enough to split stone. Wes's heartbeat thunders in my ears like a drum, too loud, too fast, layered with the scent of his fear.

"Gray!" Wes shouts, and I hear him running. "Help! Someone help!"

The world tilts sideways. Every sound becomes a symphony—the wind through leaves, insects in the soil, Wes's frantic breathing, footsteps pounding toward us from the sanctuary. I can smell each person approaching: Stellan's scent like expensive cologne and something darkly sweet that must be what an incubus carries, Thane's distinctive lack of heartbeat that marks him as vampire.

My vision blurs as my skull reshapes itself. Not breaking—expanding. Making room for senses I've never had, instincts I've kept buried so deep I almost forgot they existed. The pain is excruciating, but underneath it runs a current of relief so strong it nearly makes me sob.

"What's happening to him?" Wes demands as they reach us.

"About damn time," Stellan says, and there's satisfaction in his voice that cuts through my agony.

Through the haze of pain, I see Thane nod once, studying me with those calculating silver eyes. Not concerned. Not trying to stop what's happening.

Almost like he approves.

"You're not going to help him?" Wes's voice cracks.

"This isn't something that can be stopped," Thane says simply. "Only endured."

The bones in my arms start to lengthen. Not breaking—changing. Like they're remembering a shape they used to hold. My teeth ache, my jaw pops and stretches, and suddenly I can taste the air in ways I never imagined.

Every molecule carries information: the iron tang of Wes's blood, the old magic soaked into the sanctuary stones, the faint trace of something wrong that clings to the building like smoke.

I try to hold on to myself, to the Gray who observes and calculates and stays in control. But that version of me feels small now, cramped, like I've been trying to fit into a space that was never meant for what I'm becoming.

My muscles tear and rebuild themselves. Tendons stretch and snap back stronger. My ribcage expands to accommodate lungs that suddenly need more air, more space. Somewhere in the distance, I hear myself making sounds that aren't quite human—growls and whimpers that seem to come from something buried so deep I forgot it existed.

The scent of earth and growing things floods my senses. I can smell the individual trees in the garden, track the path of every small animal that's passed through in the last day, feel the pulse of life that runs through everything around me like a heartbeat I can finally hear.

The pain reaches a crescendo that whites out my vision completely.

Then it stops.

The agony cuts off like someone flipped a switch, leaving behind a calm so profound it's almost shocking. My breathing slows, deepens. The frantic energy that's driven me for months—the constant need to pace and watch and catalog threats—simply vanishes.

I feel right for the first time in my life.

Whole in a way I never knew I wasn't.

I push myself up from the ground, and my body moves with an easy grace I'm not used to. The world looks different now—sharper, more detailed. I can see the individual threads in Wes's shirt, count the freckles across his nose, track the rapid flutter of his pulse beneath his skin.

Colors are richer, sounds have texture, and every scent tells a story. The garden isn't just beautiful—it's alive in ways I never understood. I can feel the roots spreading beneath the soil, sense the slow growth of bark on trees, hear the whispered conversations of leaves in the wind.

"Gray?" Wes whispers.

I turn to look at him, and his eyes go wide. Whatever he sees in my face makes him take a step back.

But it's not fear. It's awe.

I try to convey that I'm fine, letting out a soft whine and tilting my head toward Wes in what I hope looks reassuring.

Stellan crosses his arms, looking satisfied. "He's fine. Better than fine. Shifter magic finally caught up with him."

"Wolf," Thane adds, and there's something like pride in his tone. "A dire wolf from the looks of it. I wondered when you'd stop fighting it."

Wes's eyes widen. "Those are the extinct ones, right?"

Stellan chuckles. "Not anymore."

A dire wolf. I can't believe it, but as the realization works through me, I feel like I might actually be able to protect the people I love.

The thought of her sends a pang through my chest, but even that feels different now. More focused. Less desperate.

I close my eyes and let my new senses expand, cataloging everything around me. The garden's living pulse, the distant sounds from the sanctuary, the way magic moves through the air like visible currents.

That's when I hear it.

A soft sound drifting from one of the sanctuary windows. At first I think it's just noise, an echo. But then the cadence registers—low, rhythmic, intimate. A sound I've heard in the dark when it was only us.

A woman's voice. Moaning.

My blood turns to ice.

I know that voice. I've memorized every sound she makes, every breath, every whispered word. It's Bree. It has to be Bree. The thought steadies me for half a heartbeat—before the sound registers for what it is. Not fear. Not pain. Pleasure. The kind of breathless, desperate sound she makes when—

"No," I breathe.

The others look at me sharply, but I'm already moving, my enhanced hearing tracking the sound to its source. It's coming from her bedroom. From the room where Jace said he was going to keep her company.

The calm I just found shatters like glass.

Because if that's really Bree—if the woman we all thought was safe and healing is making those sounds with Jace—then what the hell happened in that chamber?

And why does something that should feel like joy leave me cold with the certainty that everything we think we know is wrong?

Chapter 6
JACE

The bedroom door clicks shut behind us with a soft finality that makes my pulse spike.

Actually alone. I can't remember the last time Bree and I were alone with a bed.

Well, there was that time I brought her all those clothes—sweaters and pajamas and that soft green blanket that reminded me of her eyes when she actually smiles. We sat on her bed while I showed her everything, but it never even crossed my mind to... Gods, she was so fragile then. So breakable. The idea of making a move would have been like kicking a wounded bird.

She's always been so careful about boundaries, about making sure we're never in a position where things could get complicated. Even that morning when she kissed me in the backyard—told me I wasn't expendable, that I was everything—she pulled back before it could turn into more. Made us holy-shit-we're-alive pancakes while she teased me about kissing being "exhausting."

And now here we are, and she's not running. She's not building walls or finding excuses to leave.

She's just… here. Standing by her bed with that new confidence I'm still getting used to, looking at me like I'm something she wants instead of something she's afraid of.

My heart hammers against my ribs. This is either the best moment of my life or I'm about to spectacularly embarrass myself.

Maybe both.

"Jace." Her voice is softer now, without the audience of the others. More vulnerable. "Thank you. For backing me up out there."

"Always, sweetheart," I say, trying for my usual grin even though my heart's doing something complicated in my chest. "Though I have to say, watching you shut down Thane's doom-and-gloom routine was pretty satisfying. Guy needs to learn when to quit while he's behind."

She sits on the edge of the bed, and the mattress dips under her weight in a way that makes this feel real. Intimate. Not some dream I'll wake up from disappointed.

I cross the room slowly, needing to have her near. When I reach her, I don't sit—just stand close enough to catch the vanilla and honey scent that always clings to her skin.

"I need to tell you something," she says looking away for a moment, and my stomach drops because that tone never leads anywhere good.

"Oh great," I say, forcing lightness into my voice. "Are you about to tell me this was all an elaborate prank? Because I should warn you, my ego's pretty fragile when it comes to a certain beautiful woman luring me into their bedroom."

But then she looks up at me with those green eyes, and there's no fear in them. No walls. Just… honesty.

"I've been thinking about this for a long time," she admits. "About us. About what it would be like to—" She stops, takes a breath. "I've wanted this. You. For longer than I was brave enough to admit."

The words make the butterflies in my stomach turn violent. In the best way. The kind that knocks all the air from your lungs and makes you wonder if you're dreaming.

"Well," I manage, voice slightly hoarse, "that's definitely not what I expected you to say. Though I'm not complaining. At all. Like, seriously, zero complaints here."

She said that without a single tremor in her voice. God, she's finally sure of herself. Finally sees what we all see.

Christ.

I sit beside her on the bed, our knees bumping together. This close, I can see the flecks of gold in her eyes, smell the vanilla and honey scent that clings to her skin. Everything about this moment feels charged, electric.

"I don't want to hurt you," I whisper, because it's the truth I've been carrying for months. The fear that's kept me from pushing, from asking for more than she was ready to give.

"You won't." She reaches up, fingers trailing along my jaw with a touch so gentle it makes my chest ache. "I trust you."

And then she kisses me.

Soft at first, tentative, like she's testing whether this is real. But when I respond—when I cup her face in my hands and kiss her back with everything I've been holding in—she makes this low, pleased sound in her throat that completely undoes me.

She tastes like mint and something sweeter. Like coming home after being lost for too long.

"Is this okay?" she asks, her hands already working at my belt, and I nod because words seem impossible right now.

"More than okay, sweetheart," I manage, studying her face. Looking for any sign of doubt.

But there's nothing. Just want and certainty.

My belt hits the floor, then her shirt comes off, then mine. Each piece of clothing falling away feels like shedding armor, like finally being allowed to touch something precious I've only been able to look at from a distance.

Her skin is warm under my hands, soft curves that feel both familiar and somehow different. Smooth in places where I remember scars.

"Hey," I pause, running my thumb along her shoulder where a faint mark used to be. "What happened to—"

"I don't know." Her eyes widen, like she's just noticing too. She looks down at her arms, her expression confused. "The chamber... maybe whatever happened there..." She trails off, touching her own skin with wonder.

Then she takes my hands, guiding them over her body with a confidence that catches me off guard—moving with a certainty I've never seen from her before.

"Don't stop," she whispers, her green eyes dark with want. "Please don't stop. Not tonight."

Something about this feels different, but I can't put my finger on what—

The thought flickers through my mind, but then her mouth is on my throat and I lose the thread of it completely.

She kisses and nips at my neck, her teeth grazing my pulse point in a way that makes me groan. Her hands slide up my chest, and then she's pushing me back against the pillows with a confidence that takes my breath away.

"Let me," she says, and there's something commanding in her voice that I've never heard before.

Wait, since when does Bree take charge like—

But then she's straddling me, her hands mapping my chest with deliberate intent, and black Ether brushes across my skin like silk. The half-formed thought dissolves like smoke, leaving only the overwhelming sensation of her touch.

"You're mine tonight," she whispers against my ear, and the possessiveness in her voice sends heat straight through me. She bites gently at my earlobe, then trails her tongue down my throat.

I try to reach for her, to touch her the way I've dreamed of, but she catches my wrists and pins them above my head. "No," she says, smiling down at me. "I want to explore first."

The Bree I know would have blushed at saying something like that, would have hidden her face in embarrassment. But this version looks me straight in the eye, unashamed, as she leans down to kiss and bite her way across my chest.

This isn't like her, something's—

Silver-threaded darkness curls around my thoughts like fog, and suddenly the concern seems silly. This is Bree finally coming into her power, finally taking what she wants. This is everything I've hoped for.

She releases my wrists and sits back, her hands moving to the button of my jeans. "These need to come off," she says with that same confident smile, and I lift my hips to help her pull them down along with my boxers.

Her remaining clothes follow quickly—pants, underwear—until we're both completely bare. She slides down my body, and I watch, mesmerized, as she takes me in her mouth without hesitation. The sight of her like this—bold, confident, owning her desire—nearly undoes me.

Her lips wrap around my cock, tongue swirling around the head before she takes me deeper. She works me with her mouth and hands, alternating between slow, teasing licks and deep, hungry pulls that make my hips jerk involuntarily.

"Bree," I gasp, but she just hums around me, the vibration making my vision blur.

When she pulls away, her lips are swollen and her smile is wicked. "I want to be on top," she says, and climbs back up my body with feline grace.

She positions herself over me, taking my cock in her hand to guide me to her entrance. She's already wet, and she sinks down slowly, taking me in completely. The moan she makes is pure satisfaction, like she's claiming something that's always been hers.

"God, you feel perfect," she breathes, starting to move with a rhythm that drives me wild. She rides me like she owns me, hands braced on my chest, head thrown back in abandon.

I try to flip us over, to take control the way I always imagined I would our first time, but she presses her hands firmly against my chest, holding me down.

"Stay," she commands, and something in her voice makes me obey without question.

She moves above me with increasing intensity, rolling her hips in a way that hits every perfect spot. I can feel her getting close, her inner walls starting to flutter around me, and I reach between us to touch her clit.

"Yes," she hisses, grinding down harder against my hand. "Right there."

When she comes, it's with a cry of triumph that echoes through the room, her body clenching around me as she takes her release. The sight and feel of her coming undone above me pushes me over the edge.

Only then does she lean down to kiss me, allowing me to thrust up into her until I follow her over the edge, spilling myself inside her with a groan of her name.

Afterward, we lie tangled together in the mess of sheets and moonlight streaming through her windows. She traces lazy patterns on my chest with her fingertip, humming something low and tuneless under her breath. Something I don't recognize.

I don't think I've ever heard her hum before.

"That was…" I start, then stop because there aren't words big enough.

"Worth the wait?" she suggests, and there's laughter in her voice. Easy, comfortable laughter that makes my heart squeeze.

"Hell yes," I say, pressing a kiss to the top of her head. "Definitely worth the wait."

She tilts her face up to look at me, and her smile is radiant.

"See?" she says, eyes sparkling with satisfaction. "I told you I wasn't going to break."

The words should be comforting. Should make me feel proud, relieved, grateful that she's finally found her strength.

Instead, something cold settles in my stomach like ice water.

Because the Bree I know—the Bree I fell in love with—has always been a little broken. It's what made her real, what made her human. The cracks in her armor were where the light got in, where she let people love her despite her fear.

That's not Bree's voice. Bree would never taunt her own fragility.

This version, lying in my arms with that perfect, confident smile, doesn't have any cracks at all.

But as I lie here feeling her Ether coil around us, I let out a breath and bask in the afterglow of finally getting my girl.

Chapter 7
STELLAN

The sanctuary doors slam open with enough force to rattle the ancient hinges.

I remain in the shadows of the hallway, deliberately apart, as the others storm through the common room like a pack of wolves scenting blood. But they're not unified in their panic—each carries their own flavor of doubt.

Rhett leads the charge, fire crackling beneath his skin, convinced something's wrong but not knowing what. Gray follows, still breathing hard from his transformation back to human form—the shift was brutal, bones cracking and reforming in reverse, but faster this time. His shifter instincts still scream warnings even in his human skin. Theo moves with the jerky uncertainty of someone fighting fragmented visions that refuse to clarify. Thane brings up the rear, silver eyes cold with calculation—he's the most convinced something's wrong.

Wes trails behind, pale and sick-looking, torn between his hunger recognizing her and his instincts recoiling. The only one who seems genuinely convinced is Jace—and that's exactly the problem.

Their certainty ranges from Thane's cold suspicion to Wes's desperate hope to Jace's complete conviction that nothing's changed. It's not a witch hunt—it's a fracture line running through the group, and she's about to exploit every crack.

But it's the sound from the bedroom that stops them cold.

Her voice, confident and sultry: "Ready for round two?"

Then Jace's breathless response: "Christ, Bree. Yes. Always yes."

Followed by her laugh. Low, satisfied, entirely too pleased with herself.

The guys exchange glances sharp enough to cut glass. Without a word, they move toward her bedroom door. I drift after them, staying back, watching. Already cataloging what I'm about to witness.

For Jace's sake, I hope I'm wrong.

Rhett doesn't knock. He kicks the door open.

The tableau that greets us is damning in its intimacy.

Jace sprawled naked against the pillows, hair mussed, chest still heaving. And straddling him, equally bare, skin flushed with satisfaction—the woman wearing Bree's face.

"Jesus Christ!" Jace jolts at the intrusion, his hands flying to her hips, trying to shield her body with his own.

But it's not Bree.

I know this with the same certainty I know my own name. Everything about her posture screams conquest rather than vulnerability. The way she doesn't scramble for covers, doesn't flush with embarrassment. She simply turns to look at us with cool assessment, like she expected this interruption.

Like she orchestrated it.

Her mouth curves in a slow, predatory smirk. Then she begins to move again—deliberately.

"Bree, what are you—" Jace's voice cracks with shock and unwilling response as she rolls her hips. His confusion is immediate—why isn't she mortified? Why is she continuing?

There's something predatory in the tilt of her head as she watches us watch them. Something that enjoys their shock, their horror at finding her like this. The real Bree would have been mortified, would have hidden behind Jace, stammering apologies.

This creature preens.

"Well," she says, voice carrying none of Bree's usual startled breathlessness as she finally stills. "This is cozy."

Rhett's hands ignite, but there's something desperate in the gesture—he knows something's wrong but can't articulate what. "What the fuck is this?"

"Rhett!" Jace startles again, now dragging a sheet half over both of them as he pulls her close, one arm moving protectively around her waist. His defense is immediate, automatic. He sees an attack on her where the others see necessary questions. "Jesus, what are you—"

"That," I say quietly from the doorway, "is not Bree."

The words cut through the chaos like a blade. Every head turns toward me, but the reactions are telling. Gray nods slightly—he suspected. Theo's eyes widen with recognition, pieces clicking together. Thane's expression doesn't change, but his stillness carries agreement. Wes looks like he might be sick. Rhett just looks confused, fire guttering.

But Jace? Jace looks betrayed.

The woman meets my gaze steadily, and for just a moment, something flickers behind her expression. Something cold and calculating.

Recognition. And perhaps the faintest hint of wariness.

Good. She should be wary.

Then she blinks, and it's gone, replaced by perfect confusion.

"Not Bree?" She tilts her head, the picture of innocent bewilderment. Her eyes widen in mock confusion, but the expression holds a beat too long—just enough to be wrong. "Then who am I, Stellan? Look at Jace." Her fingers stroke through his hair with possessive gentleness, marking territory. "Does he think I'm anyone else?"

The gesture is deliberate. Intimate. Designed to use their connection against his judgment.

Jace's jaw sets stubbornly, protective fury overwhelming any doubt. "She's fine. She's safe, she's herself—stop attacking her!"

"Jace," Gray says carefully, and I can hear the weight of his own suspicions finally finding voice. "Doesn't she seem different to you?"

"Different how?" Jace's brow furrows, genuine confusion in his voice.

Her Ether, black and fluid, curls around them both as if content.

His face sets with sudden determination. "The only thing wrong," Jace continues, louder, drowning out whatever doubt was forming, "is you all barging in here like she's some kind of threat. She's been through a lot. Maybe give her five minutes to—"

"You know as well as we do," Theo interrupts, his voice carrying unusual urgency, "by the time we reached the chamber, whatever happened had already happened. And now she's here, but whoever this is, isn't acting like Bree."

For the briefest moment, uncertainty flickers across her features. A crack in the performance.

Then she leans into Jace, voice soft and wounded. "I don't remember everything. It was... overwhelming. But I'm here now. I'm safe." She looks up at him with perfect trust, eyes wide and vulnerable. "You kept me safe."

The manipulation is flawless. She's turned their reunion into proof of his protection, his worth. Made him complicit in defending her.

And that's when I see it.

Black Ether threaded with silver, unfurling like smoke. It moves with purpose, seeking targets with predatory intelligence. The inversion of everything Bree's Ether should be—darkness laced with light instead of light touched by shadow.

Rhett first—the one most confused by his own instincts. The dark threads wind around his wrists, and I watch his expression shift like a mask falling away. The fire beneath his skin gutters. His shoulders drop. "She... she looks okay." The confusion in his voice is immediate, crushing.

Then Theo—the one whose visions threatened to expose her. The mist brushes his temples, and his eyes lose their sharp focus. "Maybe the visions were symbolic," he mutters, pressing a hand to his forehead like he's fighting a headache. His gift, suppressed.

Gray she handles more carefully—his resistance is stronger, his shifter instincts harder to subvert. The threads circle him like a predator testing defenses before finding the crack: his guilt about failing to protect her. The tension bleeds from his posture slowly. "If Jace says she's fine..."

Wes simply deflates the moment the darkness touches his chest, his desperate hope winning over his Feeder instincts. "I knew it was her." The relief in his voice is heartbreaking—he genuinely believes he's found her again.

But when the mist reaches for Thane, something entirely different happens. The threads don't just hesitate—they recoil. Like they've touched something that burns them.

Thane's silver eyes remain sharp, calculating, completely unaffected. Whatever just happened, he felt nothing. But he's smart enough to play along. His posture relaxes slightly, just enough to seem influenced. For a breath, his gaze flickers—not at her, but somewhere else. Like he hears something we can't. "Perhaps we're being paranoid," he says, but I catch the deliberate choice of words. Perhaps. Not conviction—calculation.

I watch it all with cold precision. The systematic suppression of doubt. The way guilt replaces suspicion the moment her power touches them. How perfectly she's turned their protective instincts against their better judgment.

And Thane's immunity—whatever caused it—proves she can be resisted. The question is how, and why him specifically.

I wait for it to reach me, but nothing comes. No tendril seeking, no threads testing. She didn't just fail to influence me, she never tried at all. Whether by mistake or instinct, she knows I won't bend.

I keep my expression neutral, give no sign that her influence failed. Better to let her think she's won completely. Let her think I'm simply uninterested. Uninvested in their domestic drama.

"There," she says, settling back against Jace with a satisfied smile. One hand strokes his hair while the other traces patterns on his chest—a double claim of ownership. "Better?"

Jace's arm tightens around her waist, and he glares at us with protective fury. "You scared her for nothing. She's been through enough."

The others begin to shuffle, embarrassed by their suspicion. Rhett clears his throat, fire extinguished completely. Theo runs a hand through his hair, looking confused. Wes wraps his arms around himself, radiating shame.

"We should let you rest," Gray says quietly. "Sorry for... barging in."

They file out one by one, expressions confused and slightly guilty. As if they can't quite remember why they were so certain something was wrong. The Ether has done its work perfectly—not erasing their memories, but making their instincts feel cruel and unworthy.

I linger in the doorway, arms crossed, studying the woman who wears Bree's face. She meets my gaze with cool triumph, one hand still moving through Jace's hair in slow, possessive strokes. Thinking she's fooled us all.

Her smile is razor-sharp. Victorious.

"Sweet dreams," I say mildly, and turn to follow the others.

The hallway is silent except for their retreating footsteps. As I step into it, my eyes catch Thane's. His expression is carefully neutral, but something passes between us—a flicker of recognition. Understanding.

He felt it too. Whatever just happened, we both know.

The smallest nod. Barely perceptible. An acknowledgment that we'll talk later, away from listening ears and manipulative mist.

I return it just as subtly, then follow the others down the hall.

I can't stop thinking about what I witnessed. The clinical precision of her manipulation. The way she turned their love for Bree into a weapon against their own instincts. How she made Jace into her shield and the others into her unwitting accomplices.

The others may forget their doubts, mist-touched and guilt-ridden.

I will not. And I don't think Thane will either.

And when her mask finally slips—as it inevitably will—I'll be ready.

For now, I simply wait. And watch. And remember everything.

Some games are not won by the first move. They're decided by the last cut.

Chapter 8
THANE

I've been avoiding her all evening.

Not difficult when she's surrounded by the others—Rhett hovering close with protective tension, Wes trailing after her like a lost puppy, even Gray keeping her in his line of sight despite the unease I saw flickering across his face earlier. They orbit her like moths drawn to flame, and none of them see the wrongness.

Or maybe they do see it, and that black mist has already convinced them it doesn't matter.

I lean against the doorway to the common room, far enough back that I'm barely visible in the shadows. Watching. Cataloging the small tells that confirm what I already know.

The way she moves through space—too confident, claiming territory rather than navigating it carefully. The laugh that comes too easily, without the hesitation Bree always carried like armor. How she touches them—possessive rather than tentative, marking ownership instead of seeking connection.

But those are observations. Behavioral tells that could be rationalized away as growth, confidence, trauma response.

What I know with absolute certainty has nothing to do with observation.

It's hunger. Or rather, the lack of it.

Bree is my bonded. The connection between us rewrote something fundamental—made her the only one who can sustain me. Mind, body, soul if I have one. Everyone else became inadequate. Unsatisfying. That's how bonds work for vampire-class Feeders. Permanent. Exclusive. Absolute.

I'd expected the bond to settle slowly. To learn the rhythm of feeding from her, to adjust to having only one source after centuries of taking what I needed wherever I found it.

Instead, standing here watching that creature move through the room, I feel nothing.

Worse than nothing. My hunger—always present, always waiting—recoils from her like she's poison. The instinct that drives me to feed, that's kept me alive for centuries, turns away in revulsion.

It's not her. My body knows it even if the others' minds have been convinced otherwise.

And her Ether. Gods, her Ether.

Black threaded with silver instead of silver touched by shadow. An inversion so complete it should be obvious to anyone paying attention. But they're not paying attention. They're too busy being grateful she's "safe," too relieved she's "back," too desperate to believe everything's fine.

Even Zira. I watched her approach the imposter earlier, saw the initial hesitation—that split-second pause where her eyes caught on the wrong-colored Ether curling around her feet. Her mouth opened, doubt flickering across her face.

Then the black mist touched her ankle, and she smiled. Relaxed. Leaned in to embrace "Bree" like the wrongness she'd felt had never happened at all.

Only Stellan sees it. I caught his eye earlier, that barely perceptible nod in the hallway outside her bedroom. Confirmation that we're not imagining this. That something fundamental has shifted, and we're the only ones who haven't been convinced to ignore it.

She laughs at something Jace says, and the sound crawls under my skin like insects. Too bright. Too easy. Too wrong.

The imposter leans into him, and I watch Jace's expression soften with trust that makes my chest tight with something between fury and grief. He has no idea. None of them do.

Except me. And Stellan.

The bond hums beneath my ribs—a constant, uncomfortable presence that's been there since the Ashen Oath. Since Bree. The real Bree. My Bree.

And right now, it's telling me she's nowhere near this sanctuary.

I push off the doorway and slip into the hallway, moving with the silence that comes naturally after centuries of practice. No one notices me leave. They're too focused on her.

My room is dark when I enter, but I catch it immediately—the pale edge of paper on the floor just inside the door. Someone slipped it underneath while I was watching the common room.

I pick it up. Three words in Stellan's precise script.

Midnight. You know where.

The old stone well behind the gardens. We've been meeting there since we first arrived at the sanctuary with Bree—back when the others were still figuring out how to exist in the same space, and Stellan and I were mapping escape routes and defensive positions like the paranoid bastards we are. Far enough from the main building that conversations stay private, close enough that we can reach the others quickly if needed.

I glance at the clock. Twenty minutes.

I tuck the note into my pocket and move back to the doorway, checking the hall one more time before I leave.

Good. Let them be distracted. Stellan and I have work to do.

The night air hits cold and clean after the stifling wrongness of the sanctuary's common room. I slip through the kitchen—dark and empty at this hour—and out the back door into the gardens. The mist that usually clings to these grounds is subdued tonight, barely visible wisps that curl away from my feet like they know I'm not who they're waiting for.

The well sits in a small clearing ringed by old stone markers, half-hidden by wild roses that haven't been pruned in decades. Moonlight catches on the crumbling mortar, turning the whole space silver and shadow.

It's always felt liminal here. Like standing at the edge between worlds.

I'm twenty feet away when pain steals my breath.

Heat flares sharp and sudden around my wrists—not external, but internal, like shackles of fire clamped tight and burning from the inside out. I stumble, one hand flying to grip my left wrist even though there's nothing there to grab. Nothing visible.

But I feel it. Brands searing into skin that's seen too much already, claiming space where bonds form and promises are written in magic and blood.

My ankles ignite next. Same sensation—shackles, burning, binding. The kind of pain that bypasses thought and goes straight to instinct.

I've felt hunger before. Centuries of it. The gnawing emptiness that comes from going too long between feedings, the sharp desperation when it gets bad enough to cloud judgment. This isn't that.

This is different. This is *her*.

My vision fractures—silver edges going static like a signal cutting out. The world tilts sideways and suddenly I'm not standing anymore, I'm on my knees on cold stone that smells like moss and old water and something older than both.

The bond screams.

Not metaphorically. Not quietly. It tears through my chest like something trying to claw its way out, broadcasting distress so loud I can't think past it. Can't breathe past it.

She's not here. She's not safe. She's hurting.

Then something shifts. A shiver races up my spine that has nothing to do with cold or fear. Heat follows—sudden, liquid arousal that definitely isn't mine. The sensation is so foreign, so completely *her*, that for a moment I'm disoriented by feeling desire while drowning in pain.

Bree.

She's alive. Conscious. And whatever's happening to her right now is complicated enough that her body can still want even while she's trapped.

The realization steadies me somehow, even as the pain continues. She's fighting. She hasn't given up.

Somewhere, Bree is suffering. And I'm feeling the echo of it carved into my bones.

My knees hit the ground, palms scraping on stone as I try to keep myself upright. Fail. The hunger surges—not for blood, not for sustenance, but for *her*. For the connection that's supposed to run both ways but right now only broadcasts terror and isolation and wrongness so complete it makes my own emptiness feel like a mercy.

Somewhere through the haze of pain, I register footsteps. Running.

Stellan.

He drops to his knees beside me, hands immediately moving to steady—one on my shoulder, the other catching my arm before I can collapse completely. His touch is warm, solid, grounding in a way that cuts through some of the static.

"Thane." His voice is sharp with urgency I've never heard from him before. "What's happening?"

I try to answer. Can't. The bond is too loud, drowning out everything except its insistent message: *Wrong. She's not here. Find her. Wrong.*

"Your wrists," Stellan says, voice sharp with alarm.

I follow his gaze down. Red marks are appearing on my skin—angry, raised welts encircling both wrists like shackles branded into flesh. As I watch, they darken, spreading up my forearms in thin lines.

"Burns," Stellan breathes. "How is this happening?"

I manage to gasp out through the pain: "Ankles too."

He shifts immediately, and I feel his hands on my legs, hear his sharp intake of breath. "Same marks. Thane, what—"

"I don't know." The words come out broken. "Bree. I feel—she's—"

Another wave of burning cuts off whatever I was trying to say.

He doesn't waste time on more questions. Just adjusts his grip, studies my face with that clinical intensity that would be unsettling if I wasn't currently being torn apart from the inside.

"It's the bond," he says quietly. Not a question. A conclusion.

I manage a nod. Breathing is hard. Thinking is harder.

"She's not here." Stellan's gray eyes are sharp, certain. "The real one. You're still connected to her, and she's—" He stops. Reassesses. "Where is she?"

I try. Fail. My legs won't support weight, and the burning in my wrists and ankles has spread up my limbs like poison in the bloodstream.

Stellan doesn't comment on the weakness. Just shifts position, taking more of my weight without making it obvious. His strength surprises me sometimes—easy to forget what he is when he moves through the world with such careful control.

"We need to find her," I manage. "The real one."

"We will." Stellan's voice is calm, certain. "But first, you need to breathe through this. Let the bond settle enough that you can think."

"It won't settle." The truth tastes bitter. "Not while she's—wherever she is. Not while that thing is wearing her face and sleeping in her bed."

"Then we use it." Stellan's eyes meet mine, and I see the strategist sliding into place behind the concern. "You can feel her. Even across distance, even through whatever barrier separates you—you're still connected. That's an advantage."

"Doesn't feel like one."

"It will." He helps me shift position, getting me seated against the well's stone base instead of collapsed on the ground. "When we need to prove she's not Bree. When we need to find where the real one is hidden. Your bond is the evidence we need."

The burning begins to ebb slightly. Not gone—just manageable. Like my body's remembering how to function around the pain instead of drowning in it.

"The others don't see it," I say quietly. "They're convinced."

"For now." Stellan settles beside me, his usual careful distance abandoned in favor of pragmatic closeness. "But manipulation has cracks. It always does. And we're going to exploit every one."

I look at him—really look—and see the same cold calculation I feel settling in my own chest. The grief and fury crystallizing into purpose.

"She made a mistake," I say.

"Several." Stellan's mouth curves in something that's not quite a smile. "Not knowing any of us have bonded with Bree. Overlooking me entirely. Thinking Jace's devotion would be enough to keep the others from questioning."

"What do we do?"

"We watch. We wait. We collect evidence." His gray eyes are steady, certain. "And when she slips—because she will slip—we make sure everyone sees it."

The bond pulses again, but quieter now. More settled. Like it heard Stellan's words and understood: *We're coming. We haven't forgotten. We won't stop.*

Somewhere across whatever distance or barrier separates us, I hope she knows she's not alone, even if she's not here.

"She'll try to isolate us," I warn. "Make us seem paranoid. Cruel."

"Let her try." Stellan stands, offering me a hand up. "I've been underestimated my entire life. It's useful."

I take his hand, let him pull me to standing. My legs hold this time, though everything still aches with phantom shackles.

"One more thing." I meet his eyes. "You weren't touched tonight. But if her Ether reaches you later—if you start to doubt what we know—"

"You'll know," he finishes. "And you do whatever it takes to snap me out of it."

"Even if you fight it."

"Especially if I fight it." His expression is serious. "The bond protects you. I have nothing but awareness. If she gets to me, I'm counting on you to remind me what's real."

I nod. "And if the bond—"

It's not a request. It's an order dressed in concern.

I nod. "Same goes for you. If you see something the rest of us miss."

"Deal."

We stand there for a moment longer, two predators in the dark, bonded by purpose and the woman we can't live without. Even if Stellan hasn't admitted that to himself yet.

Then Stellan steps back, composure sliding into place like armor. "We should return separately. Can't give her any reason to suspect we're coordinating."

"I'll wait here. Clear my head."

He nods once, then melts into the shadows with that unnerving grace of his. Gone so completely it's like he was never there at all.

I'm alone with the well and the darkness, and somehow the solitude is comforting. The bond still burns quiet beneath my ribs, but now I can feel the echoes of Bree like they're a part of my soul.

The imposter thinks she's won. Thinks she's claimed Bree's place so thoroughly that no one will question it.

She's wrong.

And by the time we're done, she'll know exactly how wrong she is.

I touch my wrist where the phantom shackles burned, feeling nothing but my own cold skin and raised scars that weren't there before. The memory lingers—pain and connection and proof that somewhere, Bree is real and alive and waiting.

We're coming, little queen.
Just hold on.

Part Two: The Devastating Truth

Chapter 9
BREE

I open my eyes to nothing.

Not darkness—nothing. The air tastes of ash and metal, burning the back of my throat. Like someone carved out the space where light should exist and left only absence behind.

I try to sit up and my hands find ground that feels wrong—too soft, like dust that's never been walked on, but cold enough to make my fingers ache. Everything about this place feels borrowed, temporary, like it's deciding whether to exist from moment to moment.

The only light comes from directly in front of me.

A mirror, tall and silver-framed, glowing with its own pale radiance. And standing in it, wearing my face—

Riley.

She looks exactly like me, but everything about her posture screams confidence I've never possessed. She stands where I was just moments ago, in the chamber, alone but looking perfectly calm about it.

"No!" The word tears out of me before I can think. "You can't—"

Riley tilts her head, studying me through the glass like I'm something curious she found. Her mouth curves in a smile that looks wrong on my face.

"Oh, but I didn't," she says, voice carrying perfectly through whatever barrier separates us.

My stomach drops. Not denial—delight.

"What do you mean you didn't?" I scramble closer to the mirror, pressing my palms against the surface. It's cold, solid, completely unyielding. "If you didn't do this, then how—"

A sound cuts through the darkness.

Not a sound—a *noise*. Something that bypasses my ears and crawls directly into my bones. Animalistic and inhuman, like a scream that's been turned inside out and left to rot in the dark.

I clamp my hands over my ears even though it isn't sound. My bones vibrate anyway.

I jerk back from the mirror, every instinct screaming at me to run. But there's nowhere to go, nothing but black stretching in every direction.

"What was that?" I whisper.

Riley's reflection shrugs, but there's something sharp in her expression now. Alert. Like she heard it too, even from wherever she is.

"The Void has residents," she says simply. "Most of them aren't friendly."

The Void.

My stomach lurches. I know this place. My Ether brought me here before—dragged Thane with me when I lost control. We were here together in this awful emptiness before Ethos threw us back.

"You put me in the Void," I breathe, horror crawling up my throat.

Riley's smile sharpens. "I told you—I didn't put you anywhere. I had nothing to do with it."

Before I can ask what she means, movement flickers at the edges of the mirror. Familiar faces rushing into the chamber—Rhett in nothing but jeans, the others close behind, all of them looking frantic and afraid.

My heart lurches. They came looking for me. Of course they did.

I press both hands against the glass, trying to get their attention. "I'm here!" I shout, even though I know they probably can't hear me. "I'm right here!"

But they're not looking at the mirror. They're looking at Riley, and the way their faces shift from panic to confusion to something like relief makes my heart feel like it's breaking.

They think she's me.

But why wouldn't they? She looks exactly like me, stands in the space I should be in, wears my face with a confidence that must seem like healing to them.

Rhett takes a step forward, and I see the exact moment he looks into the mirror. His expression changes—just for a second, something uncertain flickering across his features. Like he's seeing something that doesn't quite make sense.

I meet his eyes through the glass, and for just a moment, I let everything I'm feeling show on my face. The terror, the confusion, the desperate need for him to understand that something is wrong.

But then Riley's reflection shifts, and whatever connection I had breaks like a snapped thread.

"See?" Riley whispers, not even bothering to look me in the eyes. "They're fine. Better than fine, actually. I can give them what they need, what you never could."

"What's that supposed to mean?"

"Certainty." She finally turns to face me fully, and there's something almost pitying in her expression. "You're always afraid, Bree. Always questioning whether you deserve them, whether you're enough, whether you'll hurt them. I don't have those fears."

"Because you don't know them!" The words come out sharper than I intended. "You don't know what they've been through, what we've built together—"

"Except this little trip to your realm seems to have given me your memories too," Riley interrupts.

Memories... she can't... that's not possible. I don't have hers.

"Memories aren't the same as—"

The mirror surface ripples, and Riley meets my eyes for a moment, a smirk on her face as she steps back, away from the glass. The connection flickers, their images growing dim.

"No, wait!" I slam my hands against the surface, but it's already too late.

The mirror goes dark, then simply... disappears.

I'm alone in the nothing.

"No, no, no," I whisper, crawling forward to where the mirror was, hands searching empty air. "Come back. Please come back."

But there's nothing. Just Void stretching in every direction, so complete it makes me dizzy. I can't tell if I'm standing or floating, if there's ground beneath me or if I'm falling through space.

I make it to my feet and stumble forward, arms outstretched, searching for anything solid. A wall, a door, another mirror—anything that might lead me back to them.

My foot catches on something, and I fall hard onto what feels like stone. Sharp edges bite into my palms, and when I pull my hands back, they come away wet with something warm.

Blood. Real blood, which means this place can hurt me.

Which means I might not be getting out.

The thought sends panic crawling up my throat, and I have to press my hand over my mouth to keep from screaming. I need to think. I need to figure out how I got here, how to get back.

But before I can form a coherent thought, a voice cuts through the silence.

"Brielle."

My name, spoken low and intimate, like a caress that turns my skin to goosebumps.

I freeze, heart hammering so hard I can feel it in my throat. I know that voice. I've heard it in dreams, felt it whisper through the dark corners of my mind when I'm trying to sleep. Heard it here, in the Void for the first time not long ago.

Ethos.

"No," I breathe, but even as I say it, part of me—some deep, secret part—responds to the sound like a flower turning toward sunlight.

"You're frightened," he continues, and I can hear amusement threading through his tone. "Lost. Abandoned by the very people who swore to protect you."

"They didn't abandon me." But my voice shakes, because what if they did? What if Riley is right, and they're better off without me? What if they prefer her certainty to my constant questioning?

"Didn't they?" Footsteps echo from somewhere in the dark, getting closer. "You called for help, and they walked away. You reached for them, and they saw only her."

"Because they don't know—"

"They don't know because they don't want to know." His voice is closer now, close enough that I can feel warmth radiating from wherever he is. "It's easier to believe you've finally become what they wanted you to be than to acknowledge what you've always been."

For just a moment, the darkness shifts. A silhouette emerges from the Void—tall, imposing, with an athletic build that speaks of dangerous strength. But it's his head that makes my breath catch: curved horns rising from a skull, pale bone gleaming against the black.

The horned mirrors. The twisted frame in the chamber.

Terror shoots through me and I stumble backward, nearly tripping over my own feet.

"And what's—what's that?" The question comes out broken, stuttered, as he melts back into shadow.

"Mine."

The word sends heat spiraling through me and ice through my veins at the same time. My knees threaten to buckle. I should run. I should fight. I should do anything except stand here letting his voice wrap around me like silk.

But there's nowhere to run in the Void.

And part of me—the part that's tired of being afraid, tired of questioning, tired of feeling like I'm never enough—doesn't want to run at all.

"Come to me, little queen," Ethos whispers, and his voice sounds like coming home. "Let me show you what it feels like to be wanted without reservation."

I close my eyes, torn between the terror of what he represents and the terrible, seductive promise in his words.

In the distance, something howls again—that same wrong, animalistic sound that makes my skin crawl.

But Ethos's voice drowns it out, warm and patient and utterly certain.

"I'm waiting," he says.

And despite everything—despite the danger, despite what I know he is, despite what choosing him might cost—I find myself taking a step forward into the dark.

Chapter 10
BREE

The ground is stone.

Then it isn't.

My foot sinks through something that shouldn't exist, and I'm falling—except I'm not. I catch myself on nothing. Literally nothing. My hand goes right through where a wall should be.

I pull back fast.

Okay. Okay. The ground changes. Don't trust it. Got it.

Except I don't got it, because I have no idea where I am or how to get out, and the darkness here isn't just dark—it moves. Breathes. I can feel it watching.

Something brushes my ankle.

A sound rips out of me—half gasp, half squeal—pure instinct. I jerk away, stumbling, skin crawling where it touched.

Not a touch. Worse. Like cold breath solidified. Like fingers that aren't fingers.

My heart slams against my ribs, but there's nowhere to go. Everywhere I turn, the black presses closer, and underneath it—

Things.

I can't see them. Can't hear them. But I know they're there. Circling. The way you know something's behind you in the dark even when you can't prove it.

My hands are shaking.

I take a step. Stone again. Then nothing. Then something that crunches but leaves no sound.

Move, my brain screams. *Don't stop moving.*

But move where? There's no direction here. No light. Just black and more black and the certainty that if I run, the things circling will chase.

Or stop, something whispers. *Just stop. Let go.*

That voice is new. Quieter than the panic, but heavier.

I shake my head hard, trying to clear it. Bad idea. The world tilts sideways, and for a second I'm falling again—not through space, through something thicker.

When everything steadies, there's light ahead.

Silver. Moving.

I stare at it, not trusting anything in this place.

The light curves through the black like—like liquid. It leaves glowing trails that fade almost immediately. It takes me too long to understand what I'm seeing.

A snake.

Silver scales catching light that shouldn't exist here. Eyes that reflect... something. I don't know what, but looking at them makes my head hurt.

I've never seen it before, but somehow it doesn't surprise me. Nothing surprises me anymore in this place.

It glides past me—not toward me, past—cutting a path through the darkness. Where it moves, the shadows pull back.

The circling things retreat.

I really don't trust it.

But when I stand still, something brushes the back of my neck. Closer than before. Close enough that I can feel the shape of teeth that haven't bitten.

Yet.

The snake keeps moving. The path stays clear.

Perfect. Follow the creepy snake or get eaten by invisible nightmare creatures.

I follow the snake.

Obviously.

I'm busy trying not to die but I notice when things start to change.

The ground stops shifting. Still black, still wrong, but solid. The things fall back further—not gone, but distant. Background static instead of trying to eat me.

My hands stop shaking.

I notice halfway through a step, and it stops me cold.

When did that happen?

I lift them, staring. My fingers are steady. Completely steady. They shouldn't be steady. Not after the mirror, or *his* voice. Not after any of this.

The cold fades next.

Not warm. Just... less. Less like drowning. Less like being crushed.

My heartbeat slows.

The panic—the choking, suffocating panic that's been strangling me since I fell—goes quiet. Not gone, but muffled. Like someone wrapped it in cotton and shoved it down deep where I can't reach it.

This should scare me.

It doesn't.

I know that's bad. I know that's really, really bad.

But the thought doesn't stick. It slides away like water off glass.

The snake glides ahead, unconcerned. Its path curves left, then right, weaving through nothing like it knows exactly where it's going.

I follow because stopping probably means the things come back.

I follow because the calm feels good.

I follow because I'm too tired to fight anymore.

Yes.

The voice. Ethos, deep and gravely resounding in my head.

Just there. Everywhere at once.

Come.

My feet move faster without me telling them to.

There's a light ahead. Like something emerging from underwater.

First, shadows that might be walls. Black stone. Maybe. Or smoke shaped like stone.

Then arches. Tall, elegant, their tops dissolving before they finish.

Silver fire runs along the surfaces. Not burning anything. Intimidating and calming at the same time. The light feels warm even though I'm not close enough to touch.

There are shapes deeper in. Low. Soft. Draped in fabric that moves even though there's no wind.

My brain tries to tell me something about that, but the thought won't fully form.

The snake reaches a clear line between the void and the half-formed chamber. It coils there, head raised.

Waiting.

Offering.

I stop.

My body's been moving on autopilot, and suddenly my brain catches up and screams.

Don't.

Turn around.

Run.

But there's nowhere to run. Behind me is teeth and hunger and circling death. Ahead is... something else. Something that whispers promises I can't hear but desperately want.

My foot lifts.

No, I think, but it's distant. Weightless.

"Yes, little queen."

His voice is in my bones now. Not sound—vibration. It spreads through my whole body until I can't tell where it ends and I begin.

"Come."

My foot crosses the line.

The calm floods in. Drowns everything. All the screaming warnings go silent under the weight of it.

Somewhere far away, I know I should be terrified.

But I can't reach that feeling anymore.

The snake uncoils and disappears in a puff of black smoke. The chamber breathes around me—welcoming, safe, home.

I take another step.

Another.

The darkness closes behind me, and I don't look back.

Something waits inside with the silver light. I can feel it watching. Patient. Absolute.

Like it's been holding its breath for me.

Chapter 11
BREE

I take two steps into the chamber before darkness wraps around my eyes.

Not a blindfold. Not fabric. Solid shadow, pressing against my face like a palm.

My hands fly up, clawing at nothing. There's nothing to grab. Just weight, heavy and absolute, blocking out everything.

Panic surges—*finally*, cutting through that unnatural calm—and my breath comes fast and sharp.

I need to see. I need to—

"Shh."

Ethos.

But his voice—it's different now. Not in my head. *Around* me.

I turn toward where I think the sound came from, spinning in the dark, but it moves. Shifts.

He's circling me.

My body starts to relax even though I'm anything but.

No. No, I need to stay afraid. Fear keeps me sharp. Fear keeps me alive. I can't let it go, I can't—

"You're safe, little queen."

What the...

Behind me now. Close.

Close enough that I feel—what? Heat? Presence? I don't know, but the air *changes* where he is. Gets heavier. Warmer.

I step forward, trying to put space between us.

The voice follows.

"You came to me." It moves again—left, then right, always circling. "So brave."

I want to argue. Want to scream that I didn't have a choice, that the snake led me, that I would've died out there.

But did I really not have a choice?

The thought slides in like oil. I could have stayed in the void. Let those things tear me apart. But I followed. I crossed the threshold.

I chose this.

Didn't I?

"You took what you wanted," he says, and each word lands with weight. Not just sound—something more. Like I can feel them settling on my skin. "What you *deserved*. They would have kept it from you forever."

The air shifts again. Closer this time.

I can feel him now. Not touching, but *there*. Like standing too close to a fire—you know it's there even with your eyes closed.

My skin prickles with awareness.

"But you reached out," he continues, voice low and approving. "You claimed it."

I try to step back.

My heel hits something solid—a wall, maybe—and I freeze.

Trapped between stone and whatever he is.

The warmth intensifies. He's right in front of me now. I know it even though I can't see. I can't hear footsteps or breathing or anything that would prove he's real.

But he is.

He's real, and he's close, and I can't move.

"They made you small." His voice wraps around me now, coming from everywhere and nowhere. "Treated you like you were less. They taught you to shrink. To apologize for existing."

Something brushes my jaw.

I flinch—but I don't pull away. Can't. My body won't obey.

The touch is light. Barely there. Could be fingers. Could be shadow.

I don't know anymore.

"They are afraid," he murmurs, and I feel breath against my ear. Warm. Real. "Afraid of what you'd become if they let you grow."

His words dig in like hooks.

Because he's right.

My father made me feel like I was something to be used. Kevin made me feel like a burden, an inconvenience. Even the guys—they want me, but they're scared too. Scared of what I can do. What I might become.

Scared of me.

"But I see you whole."

Something trails down my arm—so light I almost think I imagined it. My skin warms where it passes.

I hate that it feels good.

"I see what they were too afraid to look at."

Another touch. The curve of my shoulder. My collarbone.

Each one measured. Deliberate. Like he's mapping me in the dark.

I should be terrified.

I *am* terrified.

But underneath the fear is something worse: I want to hear more.

Want him to keep talking. Keep telling me I'm not broken. That I'm strong instead of damaged.

"They fear you," he says, and the voice is velvet now, soft and suffocating. "I will worship you."

My breath catches.

That's—

Yes.

What I deserve.

And he knows it.

"Every scar you carry…" Something traces my forearm—the one I got at twelve, defending myself from Kevin's belt. Light pressure, following the raised line. "Proof of your strength. Not your weakness."

The touch moves to another scar. The one on my ribs where Phil shoved me into the counter. Then my shoulder—the door I couldn't get through fast enough.

He knows where they all are.

How does he know?

My throat tightens.

"They marked you because they were afraid." His voice drops lower, intimate. "Each one a battle you survived. Each one proof you're still standing."

No one's ever—

No one's ever said that before.

Everyone looks at my scars and sees damage. Something to fix or pity or fear.

He sees victories.

The warmth presses closer. I can feel him everywhere now—in front, behind, surrounding. Not touching, but there. Undeniable.

"From the moment you woke," he continues, circling again, "I felt it. That power. That light in the dark."

Another touch at my temple. Trailing down to my jaw.

So gentle it almost feels like care.

"They want to tame you." The voice is right at my ear again. "Shape you into something manageable. Safe."

A pause. Heavy with meaning.

"But you were never meant to be safe, little queen."

His breath ghosts across my neck.

"You were meant to be *free*."

The word hooks into my chest and *pulls*.

What does free even mean anymore? I haven't been free since I was seven. Maybe never.

My hands are shaking. Not from fear this time.

From something I don't want to name.

"Say the word." His voice wraps around me like a blanket. "Say no, and I stop. I leave you in peace."

Silence.

Long enough that I could speak.

I don't.

Can't.

The word won't come.

"But say yes…" He's closer now. I can feel it—the heat, the presence, the weight of him in the space. "Say yes, and I show you what you could be. No more fear. No more fighting. No more pretending you're less."

Something touches my cheek. Wiping away wetness I didn't know was there.

I'm crying.

When did I start crying?

"You don't have to be strong here," he murmurs, and there's something almost tender in it. "You don't have to prove anything."

My chest aches.

I'm so tired.

Tired of being afraid. Tired of fighting. Tired of wondering if I'm too broken to fix.

"Just let go." The words are a caress against my ear. "Let me show you what you are."

My mouth opens.

The word forms, heavy and inevitable.

Yes.

One breath. One syllable.

And it ends.

All of it.

The fear. The exhaustion. The constant weight of trying to hold myself together.

I could just… stop.

"You've been so strong for so long." His voice is everywhere now, wrapping around me, pressing in. "Give it to me. I'll hold it for you."

My lips part wider.

Yes—

Something stops me.

Not panic. Not fear.

Something smaller. Quieter.

A voice that sounds like me before everything broke.

If you say it, you can't take it back.

My breath catches.

The word sticks in my throat—caught between yes and no, between surrender and something else.

I stand there, trembling.

Silence.

Then he laughs.

Low. Pleased.

For just a second, the sound is *wrong*. Too sharp. Too hungry. Like something with teeth slipped through the velvet.

But then it smooths out again, back to patience and warmth.

"Forgive me." There's amusement threading through the words now. "You make me eager. But I will not rush you."

The presence retreats. Just slightly. Giving me space I didn't ask for.

"Soon, then." The voice curls around me one last time. "We have time, little queen. All the time you need."

Breath against my ear—warm, deliberate, lingering.

"I am very, very patient."

The darkness lifts.

All at once, like someone pulled back a curtain, and I'm standing in the chamber.

Alone.

Except I'm not.

I can still feel where he touched me. Ghost touches on my jaw, my arm, my scars.

The warmth of his breath lingers at my ear.

And my pulse—it's still slowing, still matching the rhythm of his voice even though he's gone.

I look down.

Shadow clings to my wrists. Faint but real, like smoke that won't dissipate.

I try to shake it off.

It doesn't move.

My other wrist has it too. When I touch my neck, I feel it there as well—cool and present.

He left pieces of himself behind.

I wrap my arms around myself, suddenly freezing despite the silver fire flickering along the walls.

The chamber is beautiful in a sick sort of way. Black stone and shadows and fire that doesn't burn. Like a bedroom and a throne room and a trap all at once.

I should run.

Find a way out.

But where would I go? Back to the void? Back to the things that want to eat me?

And even if I could leave—even if there was a door—

Part of me doesn't want to.

Part of me wants him to come back. Wants to hear him say I'm strong again. That I'm whole. That I'm not broken.

I hate that part of me.

But I can't kill it.

I sink onto something soft—a chair or couch draped in silk—and press my hands to my face.

The shadow on my wrists brushes my cheeks. Cool. Present.

Watching.

Then—

A scent drifts across the room.

Faint. So faint I almost think I imagined it.

Smoke. Frost. Stone.

Thane.

My head snaps up, heart suddenly racing for a different reason.

But there's nothing. No one.

Just me and the silver fire and the shadows.

The scent fades as quickly as it came, like it was never there.

But I felt it.

For just one moment, I smelled him.

And I don't know if that makes this better or so much worse.

Somewhere beyond the chamber, distant and muffled, I hear it.

The Nightmare.

That sound that bypasses ears and goes straight to bone. Animalistic. Inhuman. Like a scream turned inside out.

It's hunting.

Chapter 12
SETH

The Void doesn't change.

I learned that the hard way about a thousand years ago. Or maybe it's been three weeks. Time's kind of a joke here.

Point is: the black stays black, the empty stays empty, and you either get used to it or you go insane.

I got used to it.

Mostly.

I used to mark time by how often I thought about food. Stopped doing that after the cravings made me try chewing on shadows. Turns out, darkness tastes like regret and nothing else.

Now I just walk. Talk to myself. Out loud, because if I don't, my voice might forget how to work.

"Left foot. Right foot. Thrilling stuff, Seth."

Sometimes you see flashes—people crossing through. They don't last. Most of them burn out before they even realize where they are, and I don't stick around to watch. What's the point? Can't help them. Can't save them.

Fuck, I can't even save myself.

Last time I followed a glow, it screamed until it turned to ash. Took me a week to stop hearing it.

Best I can do is not become another pile of ash myself.

My breath catches, something just shifted.

I stop mid-step, which is stupid because I wasn't going anywhere any-way. There's nowhere *to* go. Just endless nothing in every direction.

But I feel it—this ripple, like someone dropped a rock in water and the wave just reached me.

"Huh."

I scan the dark out of habit. Not that there's ever anything to see.

Except—

There.

A flicker. Silver. Gone before I can blink.

My chest does something weird. Tight. Unfamiliar.

Oh.

That's what hope feels like.

I'd almost forgotten.

"Great," I mutter. "Now I'm hallucinating."

But the feeling doesn't fade. It digs in, hooking under my ribs and pulling. Not metaphorically—my skin prickles like I brushed up against static. Like something out there already has a hand wrapped around my ribs and is *tugging*.

The air shifts. Just slightly. Carries something it shouldn't—a scent. Clean. Sharp. Like ozone after lightning.

I freeze.

That's new.

Not Ethos. I'd know that bastard's presence anywhere—feels like drowning in oil. This is different. Cleaner. Almost... warm.

Someone's here.

Someone new.

I laugh. It comes out bitter and sharp. "Oh, you poor idiot."

Whoever just crossed into the Void has no idea what they walked into. Ethos is probably already circling, deciding whether to play nice or go straight for the throat.

Smart move would be to keep walking the other way. Let whoever it is deal with Ethos on their own. Maybe he'll be busy enough that he forgets about me for a while. Let someone else bleed first.

If Ethos is already on them, maybe I can use the distraction. Get closer without him noticing me for once.

That's how I've survived this long—by being invisible, insignificant, not worth his attention.

But that pull in my chest won't quit.

And the thing is—I've seen a lot of people cross through. Watched them flicker and fade like dying stars. None of them ever felt like *this*. None of them made the Void itself react.

None of them smelled like lightning.

This is different.

This is *power*.

I run a hand through my hair, which probably looks like hell by now. Not that there's anyone around to care.

"Alright, mystery person," I say to the dark. "Let's see what you've got."

I start walking toward where the light was.

Probably a terrible idea.

Definitely a terrible idea.

But at least it's *something*. Best case, I get answers. Worst case, I finally stop walking in circles.

Either way, at least I won't die bored.

The pull gets stronger with every step, dragging me forward like a current I can't fight. My pulse kicks up—another thing I'd almost forgotten I could feel.

Then it jerks hard enough to make me stumble.

I catch myself, breathing harder than I should.

Whatever's out there isn't just calling me.

It's *dragging* me.

I keep walking. Because what else am I going to do—stay safe?

Chapter 13
BREE

I'm shaking.

Can't stop.

My hands won't stay still, my breath won't even out, and the cold—

It's not cold. The Void isn't cold. But I feel it anyway, crawling up my arms from the shadow marks on my wrists.

I try to rub them off.

They don't move.

I scrub harder, nails digging in, but the shadow just *sits there* like it's part of my skin now.

Like he marked me.

Claimed me.

I almost said yes.

The thought hits and I double over, pressing my forehead to my knees.

I almost gave in. Almost let him—

"Stop," I whisper. "Stop thinking about it."

But I can't.

Because part of me *wanted* to say yes.

Part of me still does.

That's the worst part. Not that I almost broke. That I *wanted* to break. Wanted the calm, the rest, the promise that I wouldn't have to fight anymore.

My chest aches.

I wrap my arms around myself, trying to hold the pieces together, but it feels useless. Like I'm already falling apart and just haven't noticed yet.

The mist curls around my ankles.

I look down, and my stomach drops.

The Ether coiling around my ankles isn't right.

It's had black threads since the first time I fell into the Void—since I pulled Thane and I into it and everything went dark. But this—

This is different.

The black isn't just threading through the silver anymore.

It's *half*.

Maybe more.

Silver and black twisted together like they're fighting for control, and I can't tell which one is winning.

"No."

I jerk back, but the Ether follows. It's mine. Part of me. And it's *wrong*.

I try to pull it back, suppress it like I try to when it gets too strong. But it doesn't obey. It keeps spiraling out, the black spreading like ink, until I can barely tell where the silver ends and the darkness begins.

My hands start to shake harder.

It's getting worse.

Being here—being trapped in his space—it's feeding the corruption or whatever this is. Making it stronger. Turning my Ether into something I don't recognize.

Or maybe it's not the Void doing it.

Maybe it's me.

Maybe every time I almost gave in, every time I wanted to say yes, the black grew a little more.

Either way, it's terrifying.

I close my eyes, trying to breathe through it, trying to calm down enough to pull the Ether back under control.

It doesn't work.

The darkness spreads, creeping across the floor, climbing the walls. I can feel it reaching, searching, like it's looking for something.

Or someone.

"Stop," I whisper. "Please, just stop—"

But my Ether doesn't listen.

It never really has.

I press my hands to the floor, nails scraping stone, and force everything I have into pulling it back. Reining it in. Making it *obey*.

The mist shudders. Flickers.

Then snaps back so fast I gasp.

The chamber goes still.

Silent.

I sit there, panting, staring at my hands.

The shadow marks are still there. But the Ether is gone. Pulled so far inside I can barely feel it anymore.

That's almost worse.

Because if I can't feel it, I can't control it.

And if I can't control it—

I don't finish the thought.

Instead, I push to my feet, legs unsteady, and look around the chamber.

Really look, for the first time since the darkness lifted.

It's beautiful in a sick sort of way.

Black stone walls, smooth and polished. Arches that curve into nothing. Silver fire flickering along surfaces without burning them.

And furniture.

A low couch draped in velvet. Cushions piled on the floor. A table carved from what looks like obsidian.

It looks like a bedroom.

My stomach twists.

This isn't a prison. Not the way I thought.

It's a cage dressed as a sanctuary.

He wants me to feel safe here. Comfortable. Like I chose this.

I move to the far wall, running my hands along the stone, searching for seams. Doors. Anything that might lead out.

Nothing.

Just smooth, unbroken stone.

I circle the entire chamber. Every wall. Every corner.

No exits.

No windows.

No way out.

The panic tries to claw up again, but I shove it down.

Think. I need to think.

But I can't focus. My thoughts keep slipping, sliding away like water through my fingers.

How long have I been here?

The question hits me suddenly, sharp and disorienting.

I don't know.

I woke up after he left, but when was that? Minutes ago? Hours?

There's no way to tell.

No sun. No clock. No sense of time passing at all.

I try to count back. Trace the moments from when I fell through the mirror to now.

But everything blurs together. The void, the snake, the chamber, the darkness, his voice—

It all runs into one endless stretch of fear and exhaustion.

I could have been here for an hour.

Or a day.

Or longer.

My breath comes faster.

If time doesn't work here—if it moves differently—then how long have the guys been searching?

Are they even searching?

The thought twists like a knife.

I saw them in the mirror. With *her*. With Riley wearing my face.

Do they know?

Do they realize she's not me?

Or are they—

My stomach lurches.

What if they're with her right now? Touching her. Talking to her. Believing every lie she tells them because she looks like me and sounds like me and they have no reason to doubt—

I press my hands to my face, trying to breathe through the nausea.

What if time's passed differently and they've already moved on? What if Riley's had days or weeks to convince them she's me, and they've just... accepted it?

What if they're *sleeping* with her?

The image hits like a fist to the gut, and I double over.

No. No, they wouldn't—

But how would they know?

She has my face. My voice. Maybe even my memories if the mirror showed her everything.

They'd have no reason to suspect.

And I'm trapped here, with no way to tell them, no way to get back, no way to stop her from—

The floor tilts under me, and I sit down hard, pressing my palms to the stone.

Breathe. Just breathe.

But I can't stop spiraling.

Because if time doesn't work, then I have no anchor. No way to know if I've been here for minutes while she's had weeks with them. No way to know if they're still looking or if they've already forgotten I'm gone.

No way to know if she's already in my bed. In their arms. Taking everything that was supposed to be *mine*.

The thought makes me want to scream.

But I shove it down. Force it back.

Because falling apart won't help.

Won't get me out of here.

Won't stop whatever Riley's doing.

I just have to survive.

Get back.

And pray I'm not too late.

"Stop it," I whisper. "Stop."

But the fear doesn't stop.

It builds and builds until I can't breathe, can't think, can't do anything but sit there and shake.

Then—

A blanket appears on the couch.

I freeze.

It wasn't there before. I know it wasn't.

But now it is. Dark velvet, folded neatly, like someone just placed it there.

I didn't hear footsteps. Didn't feel anyone enter.

But someone did.

Or something.

I stare at it, heart pounding.

It's just a blanket.

But it feels like so much more than that.

It's a reminder. A message.

I'm watching. I'm always watching.

I want to throw it across the room. Burn it. Destroy it.

But I don't move.

Because part of me—the part that's exhausted and cold and so tired of fighting—wants to wrap it around myself and pretend it's comfort instead of control.

I hate that part of me.

But I can't kill it.

I push to my feet, turning away from the couch, and that's when I see it.

The mirror.

Full-length, framed in black iron, standing against the far wall.

It wasn't there before either.

Or maybe it was, and I just didn't notice.

I approach slowly, warily, like it might bite.

My reflection stares back.

I look... wrong.

Paler than I should be. Hollow-eyed. The shadow marks on my wrists stand out stark against my skin.

And my eyes—

There's something in them I don't recognize.

Something darker.

I lean closer, searching for the girl I was before all this. Before the Void. Before Ethos.

She's not there.

Or maybe she is, but buried so deep I can't see her anymore.

The mist flickers at the edge of my vision—silver threaded with black—and I jerk back.

The mirror stays still.

But I swear, for just a second, my reflection smiled.

I stumble backward, pressing a hand to my mouth.

This place is breaking me.

Not all at once. Not violently.

Slowly. Gently. Like erosion.

And I don't know how to stop it.

I sink down onto the floor, back against the wall, and pull my knees to my chest.

Time passes.

I think.

I don't know how much.

At some point, I fall asleep. Or maybe I just close my eyes. It's hard to tell the difference here.

When I open them again, there's something on the table.

Clothing.

I stare at it for a long moment, not moving.

It wasn't there before. Just like the blanket. Just like the mirror.

He's been here. Or sent something. While I was sleeping or not looking or—

I don't know.

I push to my feet slowly, approaching the table like it might explode.

The fabric is dark. Almost black, but with a hint of deep purple when the silver firelight catches it. Soft. Beautiful in a way that makes my stomach turn.

I reach out, fingers brushing the material.

It's silk. Or something like it. Smoother than anything I've ever touched. The kind of fabric that costs more than I've ever had.

There's a dress. Long, flowing, with a neckline that would sit just off my shoulders. And underneath it, simpler clothes—a shirt, pants, both in the same dark, beautiful fabric.

He wants me to wear this.

Wants me to look like I belong here. In this chamber. In this cage dressed as sanctuary.

My fingers curl into the silk, and for a second—just a second—I imagine it. Putting it on. Feeling that softness against my skin instead of the rough, torn clothes I'm wearing now.

It would feel good.

That's the worst part. It would feel *good*, and he knows it.

I jerk my hand back like I've been burned.

"No."

The word comes out harder than I expected. Louder.

I grab the clothing—all of it—and throw it across the room.

It lands in a heap near the far wall, dark fabric pooling on black stone.

"No," I say again, to the empty chamber. To him, wherever he's watching from. "You don't get to dress me like a doll. You don't get to—"

My voice cracks.

I press my hands to my face, breathing hard.

He's trying to make me comfortable. Trying to make this feel like a choice. Like I'm *staying* instead of trapped.

And I almost fell for it.

Almost touched that beautiful fabric and thought about how nice it would feel.

But I won't.

I won't let him erase me like that. Won't let him replace who I am with who he wants me to be.

Even if my clothes are torn and dirty and wrong for this place.

Even if that silk would feel like heaven.

I won't.

I sit back down on the floor, as far from the discarded clothing as I can get, and wrap my arms around myself.

The chamber breathes around me.

Silent.

Watching.

I try counting again to keep myself grounded. One, two, three, four—

I lose track at thirty-seven.

Start over.

Lose track again.

My Ether pulses, unstable, and I shove it down before it can flare.

But holding it back *hurts*. Like trying to hold my breath underwater for too long.

I can't keep this up forever.

Eventually, something's going to break.

I just don't know if it'll be my magic or me.

I press my forehead to my knees and try to think of the guys. Their faces. Their voices.

But the memories feel distant. Blurred.

Like I'm already forgetting.

"Please," I whisper into the silence. "Please find me."

But no one answers.

Just the chamber, breathing around me.

And the endless, stretching dark.

Chapter 14
BREE

I wake to the feeling of being watched.

My eyes snap open, and I freeze.

He's here.

Sitting in one of the chairs near the couch, perfectly still, watching me.

I scramble backward instinctively, pushing myself up against the wall, heart slamming in my chest.

"Easy," he says softly. "I'm not going to hurt you."

His voice is the same—velvet and smoke, patient and absolute. But seeing him—

Actually seeing him—

My breath catches.

He's beautiful.

The thought hits before I can stop it, and I hate myself for it immediately.

But I can't look away.

Sharp jawline. High cheekbones. Full lips that curve slightly like he knows a secret I don't. Dark hair falls across his forehead in a way that looks deliberately tousled—like he just ran his hands through it.

And his eyes.

Forest green. Deep enough to drown in. They hold me in place even though every instinct screams to run.

He looks human. Elegant. Refined.

Devastatingly beautiful in a way that feels designed to disarm.

And I realize with a sick twist in my stomach: this is the real mask.

The voice, the darkness, the seduction—those were preparation. But this? His face? This is the weapon he uses when he wants someone to stop fighting.

Our eyes meet—really meet—for the first time, and something shifts in his expression.

Warmth. Recognition. Like he's been waiting for this moment.

"There you are," he says softly. "I was beginning to wonder when you'd wake."

I press harder against the wall, trying to put distance between us even though there's nowhere to go.

He doesn't move. Just watches me with those green eyes, patient and still.

"How long—" My voice comes out rough. I swallow and try again. "How long was I asleep?"

"Does it matter?" He tilts his head slightly. "Time doesn't work the same here. You could have slept for minutes or days. There's no way to know."

The casual cruelty of it lands like a blow.

He stands, and I tense, but he doesn't come closer. Just moves to the table where I threw the clothing.

He picks up the dress, fabric pooling in his hands like liquid shadow.

"You rejected my gift." His tone is soft. Almost hurt.

I don't answer.

He looks at me, and there's something in his expression—disappointment, maybe. Like I've genuinely wounded him.

It's a lie. I know it's a lie.

But my chest still tightens with something that feels horribly like guilt.

"I only wanted you to be comfortable," he continues, running his fingers over the silk. "To feel beautiful. Was that so terrible?"

"You're trying to control me," I manage. "Make me into—"

"Into what?" He sets the dress down gently, turning to face me fully. "Someone who feels worthy? Someone who knows her own value?"

He takes a step closer.

I press back harder, but there's nowhere to go.

"You would look exquisite in this," he says, gesturing to the dress. "The color would bring out your eyes. Make your skin glow against the dark fabric."

His voice drops lower, more intimate.

"The way the neckline would frame your shoulders... I'd watch you move in it and forget to breathe."

Heat crawls up my neck, and I hate that I feel it. Hate that his words land somewhere soft and vulnerable.

"You're already beautiful, little queen." He moves closer again—close enough now that if I reached out, I could touch him. "But imagine... feeling beautiful. Knowing it. Wearing it."

I should stand. Move away. Put real distance between us.

But I'm frozen against the wall, legs still bent where I woke, and he's right there.

Close enough that I can smell him—something clean and sharp, like spice and smoke.

It's almost intoxicating.

"I could dress you in silk every day," he murmurs. "You'd never wear anything rough again. Never feel anything but softness against your skin."

My hands curl into fists.

"You deserve that. Luxury. Comfort. To be worshipped the way you should be."

"Stop," I whisper.

But he doesn't.

Instead, he crouches.

Slow. Deliberate.

Until we're eye level.

Until those green eyes fill my entire world.

"You have scars." His gaze traces down to my arms, where old wounds mar the skin. "Beautiful scars. Proof of your strength. But you hide them. Cover them. Like you're ashamed."

He leans in slightly.

"I would kiss every one. Trace them with my fingers. Show you how perfect they are."

My breath hitches, and his eyes flicker with satisfaction.

"May I?" he asks, lifting one hand slowly.

I should say no.

Should pull back, refuse, keep the distance.

But I'm so tired.

And his voice is so soft.

And part of me—the part I hate—wants to know what his touch feels like when I can see his face.

I nod.

Just barely.

His fingers brush my jaw, feather-light, and I shiver.

He traces the line of my cheekbone. Tucks a strand of hair behind my ear. His touch is gentle. Reverent. Like I'm something precious.

"You're shaking," he murmurs. "Are you afraid of me? Or afraid of this?"

I don't answer.

Can't.

His thumb brushes across my lower lip, and my breath stutters.

"Your reflection in the mirror," he says softly, "she knows her worth. Wears it like armor."

The mention of Riley makes my stomach drop.

"You could too," he continues. "If you let yourself."

I pull back slightly, and he lets me. Doesn't chase.

Just watches with those green eyes that see too much.

"She's not afraid to take what she wants," he says. "To be powerful. Beautiful. Desired."

The comparison twists like a knife.

Because he's right.

Riley looked confident. Certain. Everything I'm not.

And the guys—

They're with her. Believing she's me. Maybe even—

"You could be like her," Ethos murmurs. "Strong. Unafraid. If you stopped fighting what you are."

His hand drops to my wrist, fingers brushing the shadow marks there.

"You wear my marks beautifully," he says, voice almost tender. "They suit you. Like they were always meant to be there."

I jerk my hand back, and he rises smoothly—standing again, giving me space I didn't ask for.

He moves back to the table. Back to the dress.

Picks it up again, holding it out toward me.

"Wear it for me," he says. "Just once. Just to see."

I stare at the fabric, dark and beautiful and wrong.

"If you hate it, you can take it off. But let me see you in it. Let me show you how beautiful you are."

My fingers twitch.

I could—

Just once.

Just to see what it feels like.

To feel beautiful. Desired. Worthy.

The way Riley must feel.

The way the guys probably see her now.

My hand lifts without me telling it to.

Reaches toward the silk.

Then stops.

No.

No.

I curl my fingers into my palm and pull back.

"I'm not her," I say, voice shaking. "And I'm not wearing that."

For a moment, silence.

Then he smiles.

Slow. Satisfied. Like I've given him exactly what he wanted.

"Tomorrow, then," he says softly.

And vanishes into shadow.

I'm left alone in the chamber, staring at the dress still draped across the table.

My hand is still trembling.

And I can't tell if it's from fear or something worse.

Chapter 15
SETH

The pull hasn't stopped.

It's been—hours? Days? Who the hell knows—since that silver light flickered through the dark, and the thing hooked under my ribs hasn't let up since.

Worse, actually.

It's gotten sharper. Tighter. Like someone replaced the thread with barbed wire and decided to yank.

I stumble over nothing—because everything here is nothing—and catch myself against empty air.

"Fantastic," I mutter. "Haunted by a ghost with better cardio than me."

I keep walking anyway.

What else am I going to do? Stop? Let the pull rip me apart from the inside? At least moving feels like I'm doing something.

Even if that something is probably walking straight into a trap.

The scent hits me again.

Ozone. Sharp. Clean.

Stronger this time.

I freeze, breathing it in like it's the first real air I've tasted in years.

It probably is.

I turn slowly, trying to pinpoint the direction, but it's everywhere and nowhere. The Void doesn't do directions. Doesn't do *anything* except crush hope and swallow light.

But this—

This is different.

The darkness around me feels... wrong. Not the usual oppressive nothing. There's a pulse to it. Faint. Like veins of light running through the black.

Silver veins.

I reach out, and the air shimmers where my fingers pass through.

"What the hell?"

I've been here long enough to know the Void doesn't change. Doesn't react. It just *is*—static, eternal, empty.

But now it's moving.

Breathing.

Alive.

And I realize: it's not the Void changing.

It's *them*.

Whoever crossed over, whatever power they're carrying—it's rewriting the rules just by existing here.

I laugh. It comes out sharp and bitter.

"Of course. Of course you're that strong."

The pull jerks hard, and I stagger forward.

Then I hear it.

Voices.

Faint. Distant. But *there*.

I stop dead, every muscle locking up.

The Void doesn't echo. Doesn't carry sound. When people scream here, it swallows the noise before it can travel.

But I'm hearing voices.

Whispers threading through the dark like they're being carried on wind that doesn't exist.

A laugh. A sob. A word I almost recognize.

"Okay," I whisper. "Now I'm officially losing it."

But I keep listening.

Because even if I'm going insane, it's the first sound besides my own voice I've heard in so, so long.

The whispers fade, but the pull doesn't.

It drags me forward, relentless, and I follow because I don't have a choice anymore.

My legs are shaking. My chest aches. I haven't rested in—

Actually, I don't remember the last time I rested.

Used to be able to. Used to find pockets of relative safety where I could stop moving for a while.

But the pull won't let me anymore.

It wants me *there*. Wherever "there" is.

And it's not taking no for an answer.

I stumble through zones scattered with ash.

Old crossings. Failed attempts. People who tried to walk through the Void and didn't make it.

I've seen this before. Too many times.

The last time I followed a light, it screamed until it turned to ash. Took me a week to stop hearing it.

But this—

This feels different.

Less like a candle burning out.

More like a wildfire spreading.

The silver veins in the darkness get thicker. Brighter. Like roots growing through stone.

And I realize: they're not fading.

They're *taking hold*.

I press a hand to my chest, trying to ease the ache where the pull digs in.

"If you're Ethos bait," I mutter, "this is a really elaborate setup."

But I don't feel his presence.

That's what's unnerving.

He should be here. Should be circling, watching, waiting to strike.

But there's nothing.

Just the pull. Just the light. Just the voices whispering through the dark.

Either he hasn't noticed—

Or he wants me to find them.

Either way, I'm already caught.

"Might as well see it through," I say to the empty black. "Hard to lose when the bar's this low."

The pull jerks again, so hard I nearly collapse.

I stumble forward, gasping, and the darkness shifts.

Thins.

That's the only word for it.

Like I've walked into a pocket where the Void is less dense. Less absolute.

The air changes. Warmer. Almost breathable.

And I hear it.

A voice.

A woman's voice.

Not a whisper this time.

Clear. Close. *Real.*

One word.

"Stop."

I freeze, breath caught in my throat.

It's her.

It has to be.

I whisper into the thinning dark:

"...Who are you?"

No answer.

Just the pull, stronger than ever.

And the certainty that I'm close.

So close I can almost feel her breath.

Chapter 16
BREE

I can't stop staring at the dress.

It's been—I don't know how long. Time doesn't work here. But since he left, since he smiled like he'd already won, I haven't been able to look away from the dark fabric pooled on the table.

It's just clothes.

Just fabric.

Nothing more.

I tell myself this over and over, but it doesn't help.

Because I'm freezing. My torn clothes are filthy, stiff with dirt and sweat and whatever else I've dragged through. My skin feels grimy. Wrong.

And that dress—

That dress looks soft. Clean. Beautiful.

"It doesn't mean anything," I whisper to the empty chamber. "Putting on clean clothes doesn't mean I'm giving in."

But even as I say it, I know it's a lie.

Everything here means something.

I push to my feet, legs unsteady, and move toward the table.

My hand hovers over the silk.

Just touch it. See if it's as soft as it looks.

My fingers brush the fabric, and it slides like water.

Softer than anything I've ever felt.

I lift the dress slowly, fabric spilling over my hands, catching the silver firelight.

It's beautiful.

And I hate how much I want to put it on.

I glance toward the mirror—still there, watching—and deliberately turn my back to it.

As if that makes a difference.

As if he isn't watching anyway.

I strip off my torn clothes, piece by piece, and the cold air bites my skin. I move fast, not letting myself think, not letting myself stop.

The dress slides over my head.

The silk caresses every inch of skin it touches—shoulders, arms, waist, hips. It clings and flows at once, like it was made for me.

Like it *knows* me.

I smooth the fabric down with shaking hands and stand there for a moment, facing away from the mirror.

My heart pounds.

I don't want to look.

Don't want to see what I've become.

But I can't help it.

I turn slowly, and my breath catches.

That's—

That's me.

But also not me.

The neckline sits just off my shoulders, framing my collarbones. The dark fabric makes my skin look luminous, my eyes brighter. My hair falls in tangled waves, but somehow it looks intentional. Wild in a way that feels powerful instead of broken.

I look... beautiful.

Dangerous.

Desired.

Like Riley.

The thought twists like a knife.

"This isn't me," I whisper to my reflection.

But she almost looks like she disagrees.

Movement in the mirror makes me freeze.

Behind me.

A figure stepping out of shadow.

Him.

My heart stops.

He moves slowly, silently, until he's directly behind my reflection. Close enough that I can see every detail of his face in the glass. Close enough that I feel the heat of him at my back.

I don't turn around.

Can't.

I'm caught between him and the mirror, and all I can do is stare at our reflections together.

His forest green eyes meet mine in the glass.

"Perfect," he says softly.

The word shivers down my spine.

He doesn't touch me. Not yet. Just stands there, both of us framed in black iron, looking at what we've become together.

His gaze travels over my reflection—slow, reverent, burning.

"Do you see?" His voice is low, intimate. "Do you see what I see?"

I can't answer.

Can't breathe.

His hand lifts slowly, and I watch in the mirror as it hovers near my shoulder.

Then settles.

Light. Careful. Like I might break.

I flinch but don't pull away.

Can't move.

His fingers trail down my arm, barely touching, grazing the silk.

"I knew it would suit you," he murmurs.

In the mirror, we look like a pair.

King and queen.

Predator and prey.

I don't know which is worse.

He tilts his head slightly, dark hair brushing near my temple as he studies our reflection.

"Look at you," he says softly. "Radiant. A queen in her own right."

His hand drifts lower, fingertips brushing one of the scars visible at my collarbone.

I tense, but he doesn't pull away.

Just traces it gently, like it's something precious.

"Even your scars adorn you," he whispers. "Proof of strength. Proof you were always meant to be more than they allowed you to be."

I feel seen.

Completely, terrifyingly seen.

And I hate that part of me *wants* this. Wants to be looked at like I'm beautiful instead of broken.

Then his hand moves.

To my shoulder. The strap of the dress has slipped slightly—barely—but he notices.

His fingers hook under the silk, adjusting it with agonizing slowness. The backs of his knuckles brush my bare skin, and I shiver.

He sees it in the mirror. His lips curve.

"Cold?" he asks, though we both know that's not why I'm shaking.

His other hand lifts, gathering my hair gently and drawing it over one shoulder. His fingertips graze the back of my neck as he moves the strands, deliberately slow, and I feel the touch like a brand.

My breath comes faster.

In the mirror, his hands hover at my waist. Not touching. Just... there. Close enough that I can feel the heat of them through the silk.

"May I?" he asks softly.

I should say no.

Should pull away, run, fight.

But I don't.

I nod.

Just barely.

His hands settle on my waist, and the contact sends heat through my entire body. Not rough. Not possessive.

Reverent.

Like I'm something sacred.

His thumbs brush the curve of my hips through the fabric, and I watch in the mirror as he leans closer, his breath warm against my ear.

"You were never meant to be less," he breathes. "You were always meant to be mine."

His eyes lock with mine in the mirror, and for one dizzying, horrible second, I can't tell if I'm terrified—

Or thrilled.

My hands rest at my sides, trembling.

Part of me wants to tear the dress off. Throw it back in his face. Scream that I'm not his, will never be his.

But another part—

Another part leans back into his touch.

Just slightly.

Just enough.

And we both see it happen in the mirror.

His smile is slow. Satisfied.

"Tomorrow," he whispers against my temple.

Then he's gone.

Vanished into shadow like he was never there.

I stand alone in front of the mirror, wearing his dress, feeling the ghost of his hands on my waist.

And I know—with a certainty that makes me want to scream—that when tomorrow comes, I won't tell him no.

Chapter 17
BREE

I wake in silk.

The dress clings to my skin like shadow, dark and unfamiliar. I never chose this. The fabric pools around me on cold stone, and when I move, it slides against me with a whisper that makes my skin crawl.

Where am I?

The chamber breathes around me—black stone walls, silver fire flickering without heat. Everything is wrong. The air tastes like smoke and frost, and underneath it all, something that makes my stomach turn.

Hunger.

I try to remember how I got here. The sanctuary. The fountain. Ethos's voice threading through my mind like silk ribbon around my throat.

"Come to me, little queen."

I must have followed. Must have walked through shadows or mirrors or whatever pathway he laid out for me. But the memory feels hazy, dreamlike. Like watching someone else's life through thick glass.

The mirror catches my attention.

It stands against the far wall—black iron scrollwork, ornate and ancient. The kind of mirror that belongs in nightmares. When I look into it, my reflection stares back, but there's something in my eyes I don't recognize.

Surrender.

The thought comes from nowhere, settling in my chest like a weight I don't remember picking up. I should be afraid. Should be fighting to get out of here. Instead, I just... exist. Suspended in this strange space between terror and something that might be relief.

I'm tired of fighting.

The realization whispers through me, and part of me—a part I don't want to acknowledge—finds comfort in it.

"You waited for me."

His voice comes from behind me, warm and intimate. I don't turn around. Can't, maybe. Or won't. In the mirror, I watch my reflection's eyes flutter closed at the sound.

Ethos moves behind me like shadow given form. I feel him more than see him—heat at my back, the whisper of breath against my neck. The silver fire along the walls pulses once—like a heartbeat beneath the stone. Then his fingers brush my shoulder, and electricity shoots down my spine.

"I told you that you would choose," he murmurs, and his voice is everything I've been missing. Certainty. Desire without apology. "Look how beautiful you are when you stop fighting."

My reflection shows me the truth. The dark silk clinging to curves I usually hide. My lips parted, breath coming quick and shallow. The hunger in my own eyes that I've been denying for so long.

I want this.

The thought should horrify me. Instead, it settles somewhere deep in my chest and stays.

His hand slides down my arm, fingers trailing electricity. Where he touches, cold shoots through me—sharp and sudden—but then it's gone, replaced by heat that makes me lean back against him.

"Tell me what you want," he whispers against my ear.

"I—" The words stick in my throat. Because I do want. I want to be desired without hesitation. I want to be chosen without question. I want to take instead of always giving until there's nothing left.

"I want to stop being afraid," I whisper.

"Then stop."

His mouth finds the curve of my neck, and my knees almost buckle. Heat floods through me, drowning out everything except the press of his lips, the scrape of teeth that should terrify me but doesn't.

In the mirror, I watch my reflection arch against him. Watch silver mist spill from my fingers, reaching for him like it's been starving.

It has been. I have been.

He turns me from the mirror, and for the first time I see his face fully. Beautiful in a way that makes my chest ache. Dark hair, sharp features, eyes that hold centuries of knowing exactly what he wants.

And right now, he wants me.

"Please—" The word slips out before I can stop it.

He smiles, and it's the most beautiful thing I've ever seen.

"Finally."

His mouth captures mine, and the world disappears.

The kiss is everything—desperate and consuming and perfect. He tastes like power and promises, like all the things I've been too afraid to want. When his tongue slides against mine, electricity shoots down my spine and settles low in my belly.

My hands fist in his shirt, pulling him closer. I can't get close enough. Can't breathe around the want that's consuming me from the inside out.

He breaks the kiss, and I actually whimper at the loss.

"Shh," he soothes, hands framing my face. "I'm not going anywhere."

The cushions appear without my noticing—soft and dark, spread across the stone floor like an altar. He guides me down, and I go willingly. Let him position me exactly where he wants me.

When he raises my wrists above my head, crossing them, something cool slides around them. I should panic. Should fight. Instead, I test the bonds and find them like silk—holding me but not hurting. Comforting in their certainty.

"Beautiful," he murmurs, and the word goes straight through me. "Do you feel it? How right this is?"

I do. God help me, I do.

His hands map my body through the silk—tracing curves, finding places that make me gasp and arch. Every touch sends lightning through my veins, and my Ether responds, silver mist curling around us both.

"More," I breathe, and I'm not sure if I'm talking to him or to the magic. He obliges.

His mouth follows where his hands led—pressing kisses to my throat, my collarbone, the swell of my breasts through silk. When he finds a particularly sensitive spot, I cry out, and the sound echoes off stone walls.

The silk slides away like water, leaving me bare and wanting. He takes his time looking at me, and under his gaze I feel powerful. Desired. Chosen.

"Perfect," he says, and it sounds like worship.

When his mouth closes around my nipple, my back arches off the cushions. Pleasure shoots straight to my core, and the bonds around my wrists tighten just enough to remind me I'm his. That I chose this. Chose him.

His hand slides between my thighs, finding me already slick and ready. I moan when he touches me, really touches me, fingers sliding through wetness to find the bundle of nerves that makes my whole body sing.

"So responsive," he murmurs against my skin. "So perfect for me."

He builds me up slowly, expertly, until I'm writhing against his hand and begging for more. When he finally slides a finger inside me, I nearly come apart.

"That's it," he encourages, adding a second finger. "Let go for me."

I can't hold back anymore. Can't think past the pleasure building inside me like a storm. When my climax crashes over me, silver Ether explodes from my skin, flooding the chamber with light.

And something else.

Streaks of ink threading through the silver like veins. Beautiful in a strange way, like shadow flowing through water. But I'm too lost in pleasure to care, too high on the feeling of being completely, utterly desired.

He doesn't stop. Doesn't give me time to recover. His mouth replaces his fingers, and I scream at the sensation. He devours me like he's starving, like I'm the only thing that will save him.

Maybe I am.

The second orgasm is even stronger than the first. My Ether surges again, silver shot through with growing ribbons of darkness. In the very back of my mind, something whispers that this is wrong. That I'm losing something with every pulse of pleasure.

But it feels so good to lose. So good to finally take what I want without apology.

When he rises over me, I spread my legs wider in invitation. He's perfect—all lean muscle and sharp edges and eyes that see straight through to my soul.

"Are you ready for me?" he asks, and there's something in his voice I can't identify. Hunger, maybe. Or triumph.

"Yes," I breathe. "Please, yes."

He enters me slowly, carefully, and I've never felt so complete. So perfectly filled. The stretch is delicious, the friction exactly what I need. When he starts to move, I meet him stroke for stroke, chasing the pleasure that builds between us.

"Mine," he growls against my throat, and the word resonates in my bones.

"Yours," I agree, because it's true. In this moment, in this place, I am completely his.

The rhythm builds until we're both desperate, both racing toward something that feels like salvation. When my third climax hits, it takes him with me. He spills inside me with a groan that sounds like victory, and my Ether explodes outward one final time.

This time, the silver is barely visible beneath the black.

But I don't care. Can't care. I'm floating on waves of satisfaction and completion, wrapped in the certainty that I've finally found where I belong.

He pulls me against his chest, and I curl into him like I was made to fit there.

"Sleep, little queen," he murmurs, lips against my hair.

My eyes flutter closed, and for the first time in forever, I feel safe. Chosen. Loved.

I don't notice the way my Ether dims with every breath. Don't feel the way my strength seeps away like water through cracks.

All I know is that I'm his now.

And that's exactly where I want to be.

I sleep, and dream of silver turning to shadow.

Part Three: Nothing Is As It Seems

Chapter 18
THEO

The vision doesn't ask permission.

One moment I'm standing in the new training hall—the one Bree insisted on yesterday, and the sanctuary reluctantly provided. It stands out, black obsidian and ancient stone, colder than the rest of the sanctuary's warm corridors. Rhett's demonstrating fire control to a group of newly arrived refugees, flames dancing between his fingers.

The next, the world tilts sideways and I'm falling through darkness that tastes like smoke and silver.

I try to fight it. I've gotten better at that—pulling back before the visions drag me under completely. But this one has hooks in deep, and when I try to surface, it just pulls harder.

Then I see her.

Bree.

She's framed in a mirror—black iron scrollwork, ornate and ancient. The kind of mirror that belongs in a nightmare, not a sanctuary.

Where is she?

She's wearing dark silk. Off-shoulder, clinging to curves I've memorized despite myself. The fabric pools around her like ink, like shadow given form. She'd never choose this. She barely owns anything silk at all, and when she does wear it, it's soft colors. Cream. Lavender. Not this.

Not black.

The stone beneath her is polished obsidian. Cold. I can feel it through the vision, radiating a chill that has nothing to do with temperature. Silver fire burns in sconces along the walls—wrong, all of it wrong. The flames don't flicker like normal fire. They pulse. Breathe. And they hum—low and unnatural, like a heartbeat beneath the stone.

She's alone in the frame.

But she's not.

Her breath catches. Shallow. Quick.

Her back arches slightly, and I watch her eyes flutter closed. Lips part. Just barely. The kind of response that comes from touch, from skin on skin, from—

I try to see who's with her. Try to shift the vision, expand it, catch even a glimpse of movement or shadow.

Nothing.

Just her. Just her face, her body responding to something I can't see.

Someone's touching her.

Why the hell can't I see who it is?

The realization hits like cold water. Someone is touching her, and she's reacting. Her shoulders tense. Her head tilts back. The silk shifts as she moves, sliding lower on one shoulder.

Then I see them.

Marks on her wrists. Dark bands circling pale skin like bracelets. Not bruises—something else. Something that moves slightly when I try to focus on it, like smoke trapped under glass. They pulse once—like a heartbeat—then go still.

I don't know what they are, but they look like shadow.

And I know they're wrong.

Her breath catches again. Sharper this time. Her fingers curl against nothing—reaching for something, or trying to push it away. I can't tell.

The silk slides lower.

Her eyes open.

For one impossible moment, she looks directly at me. Through the mirror. Through the vision. Through whatever barrier separates us.

Her green eyes staring right into my soul.

And she's terrified.

But there's something else in her eyes. Something that makes my stomach turn and my body respond in ways that fill me with shame.

Desire.

Need.

Surrender wrapped in fear wrapped in want.

"Please—" she whispers.

A tremor runs through me—not fear, something deeper. I smell smoke and silver, feel the ghost of her breath against my skin even though I'm not there. A sound echoes through the vision—soft, wordless, unmistakably hers.

The vision shatters.

Nausea hits first—sharp and immediate, crawling up my throat. Then the heat. My body is responding, arousal and revulsion tangled so tightly I can't separate them. The room spins as I stumble backward, and strong hands catch my shoulders before I hit the floor.

"Easy." Thane's voice. Cold and controlled. "I've got you."

I try to focus. The training hall comes back in pieces—polished wood floors, afternoon light streaming through high windows, the distant sound of Rhett's voice still explaining something about flame control.

My body is shaking. I'm hard.

Disgusted with myself.

"Vision?" Stellan's voice, quiet enough that only Thane and I can hear.

I nod once, not trusting my voice yet.

Thane's grip on my shoulder tightens briefly, then releases. "Can you walk?"

Another nod.

"Come on." He guides me toward the far corner of the hall—away from Rhett's demonstration, away from the refugees, into shadow where we won't be overheard.

Stellan follows, moving with that elegant silence of his.

I catch Wes watching us from across the room. His eyes are wary, tracking our movement. He knows something happened, but he's too consumed with his own unfulfilled hunger to press.

And there—padding through the far door—Gray in his wolf form. White fur, massive, surrounded by other shifters. They're laughing at something, the wolves play-fighting while the humans watch. It's almost cute, seeing Gray like this. Relaxed. Part of a pack.

He doesn't notice us slip away.

None of them do, not really.

Thane positions himself between me and the rest of the hall, blocking their view. Stellan leans against the wall, arms crossed, expression unreadable.

"What did you see?" Thane asks quietly.

I force myself to breathe. To organize thoughts that feel scattered and wrong.

"A mirror," I manage. My voice sounds wrecked. "Black iron. Ornate."

"Where?" Stellan asks.

"I don't know. Stone floors. Obsidian, maybe. Silver fire on the walls."

Thane goes very still. I feel it—the sudden tension, the way his breathing stops for just a moment.

"She was wearing dark silk," I continue, the words tasting like ash. "Off-shoulder. Black. She'd never—she wouldn't choose that."

"What else?" Stellan's tone is careful now. Too careful.

"Marks on her wrists." I swallow hard. "Shadow marks, I think. Circling like bracelets. They moved. Pulsed once, like a heartbeat. I don't know what they are."

Silence. The kind that feels heavier than sound.

"Was she alone?" Thane's voice has dropped lower. Dangerous.

"I—" The memory makes my throat close. "No. Someone was touching her. I couldn't see who. Just her reaction. Her face. Her body…"

I can't finish. Can't explain the way she moved, the way she surrendered. The horrifying intimacy of watching her pleasure without understanding its source.

"Was she afraid?" Thane asks.

"Yes." The word tastes bitter. "Terrified. But also…"

I can't finish. Can't admit what else I saw in her eyes.

Stellan finishes for me. "Desire."

The reality of it makes me flinch. But he's right. That's exactly what I saw. Terror and desire mixed in a way that one feeds the other.

"That's not Bree," Thane says. No emotion. Just fact.

"It looked like her," I protest, but even as I say it, doubt creeps in. Because he's right. The woman I saw—the way she moved, the doubt even in surrender, the dark silk she'd never choose—

But also... it *was* her. I know her face. Her body. The way her eyes look when she's scared.

"I don't know," I admit finally. "It looked like her. Felt like her. But everything else was wrong."

"The marks," Stellan says. "You're certain they were shadow marks? Not bruises or bindings?"

"They moved." I try to visualize them again, but the memory is already starting to blur the way visions do. "Like smoke, circling her wrists but not touching. I've never seen anything like them."

Stellan and Thane exchange a look. A long one. The kind of communication that happens between people who've known each other for centuries and don't need words anymore.

"What?" I demand. "What do those marks mean?"

"Nothing good," Stellan says finally. "But if that's what I think they are—"

"Then wherever the real Bree is," Thane interrupts, "she's in deeper trouble than we thought."

The real Bree.

The words hang between us like a death sentence.

"You think—" I can't finish. Can't voice what they're suggesting.

"I think," Thane says carefully, "the woman walking around this sanctuary is playing a part. And she's very good at it. And I think whoever you just saw—wherever she is—is the real one."

My stomach drops.

"Then where is she?" The question breaks out of me, raw and desperate. "If that's the real Bree, where is she? What's happening to her?"

"I don't know," Thane admits. His silver eyes are cold, calculating. "But your visions might be the only way to find out."

The responsibility of it settles over me like a weight.

"The others don't believe you," I say quietly. Not a question. A fact.

"No." Stellan's expression doesn't change. "They think we're paranoid. That Bree's just grown stronger after the Oath. More confident. More... herself."

"But you don't think that."

"I *know* that's not her," Thane says flatly. "I've known since she came back. The way she looks at me. The way she moves. It's almost perfect. But it's not Bree."

"And you want me to keep watching." My voice comes out hollow. "Keep having these visions. Keep seeing her—whoever she is—being touched by something I can't identify."

"Yes," Thane says simply.

"Even though my body responds." The confession tastes like bile. "Even though I'm aroused watching her—"

"That's not your fault," Stellan says, and there's something almost gentle in his tone. "Visions aren't passive observation. They pull you in. Make you feel what the subject feels."

"She was terrified," I say, looking up at him. I know he can see the shame in my eyes. "And aroused. And I felt both. But my body only responded to one."

"Because that's what she was feeling strongest," Thane says quietly. "You're not aroused by her fear, Theo. You're responding to her desire. To her pleasure. That's what the vision showed you most clearly."

"While someone I can't see touches her," I whisper. "While she's trapped somewhere and I just—I just watch and feel—"

"You're seeing her," Stellan interrupts. "That's what matters. You're the only thread we have to wherever she actually is."

Across the hall, Rhett's demonstration is wrapping up. The refugees are dispersing. Soon they'll notice us huddled in the corner, notice the tension crackling between us.

"What do I tell them?" I ask quietly. "When they ask what happened?"

"Nothing," Thane says immediately. "Not yet. If the others think something's wrong—if they start questioning her—whoever's wearing Bree's face will know we're onto them."

"So we just pretend everything's fine?" The bitterness in my voice surprises even me. "While the real Bree is trapped somewhere being—" I can't finish.

"While we gather information," Stellan corrects. "While we use your visions to figure out where she is and how to get her back."

"And if I'm wrong?" The question comes out broken. "What if these visions are just my fears? My desires twisted into nightmare? What if I'm seeing what I'm afraid of instead of what's real?"

"Then we'll figure that out too," Thane says. His silver eyes meet mine, and for once there's something almost gentle in his expression. "But right now, those visions are all we've got."

I close my eyes, trying not to see her face. Her fear. Her need. The way she looked directly at me without recognition, like I was just another shadow in her nightmare.

"Okay," I say finally. The word tastes like surrender. "I'll keep looking."

Even if it destroys me.

Even if every vision drives the guilt deeper.

Even if I never wash the shame of being aroused by her suffering.

I'll keep looking.

Because if I don't—if I let fear or shame stop me—then she's lost.

And I can't live with that.

Thane nods once. Stellan's expression doesn't change.

"One more thing," Stellan says as we prepare to rejoin the others. "Don't tell Wes. Not yet."

"Why not?"

"Because he's already unstable," Thane says bluntly. "His feeding patterns are erratic. His control is slipping. If he knows the real Bree is trapped somewhere, being touched, he'll spiral."

I remember the way Wes looked earlier. The wary watching. The tension in his shoulders.

"He already suspects something," I say.

"Let him suspect," Stellan replies. "But don't confirm. Not until we know more."

I nod slowly.

We step back into the light of the training hall. Rhett waves us over, grinning about something. The wolves are still playing in the corner—Gray's white fur bright among the others.

Everything looks normal.

Everything feels wrong.

And somewhere—in a mirror, in a place I can't reach—Bree is terrified and surrendering while someone I can't see touches her.

When I close my eyes, the mirror flashes behind my eyelids.

Just for a breath.

Just long enough to see shadow chains wrapped around pale wrists, tightening until they disappear into darkness.

Chapter 19
WES

The sanctuary gardens feel hollow in the moonlight.

I sit on the low stone wall beside what used to be flower beds, watching silver light spill across my hands. The Ether should respond to me here—Bree's magic is woven into every stone, every blade of grass. But when I reach for it, there's nothing. Just the familiar ache gnawing at my ribs.

The first time I fed from her, I felt complete. Not just satisfied—*seen*. Like every hungry, desperate part of me finally had a place to rest. She touched me and I understood what it meant to be chosen instead of tolerated.

Now everything feels like echoes.

She kissed me today. Told me she missed me. But when her lips touched mine, I felt nothing. Or maybe I felt everything she wasn't giving me. The warmth was there, the softness, but underneath it—silence. Like kissing a beautiful reflection that can't kiss back.

I don't understand what's changed. Don't understand why the hunger has gotten worse instead of better. Don't understand why I feel more alone now than I did before she ever touched me.

Distant laughter drifts from the sanctuary windows. Probably Rhett telling one of his stories, or maybe Theo reading something amusing aloud. Normal sounds. Comforting sounds.

Sounds that make me feel like I'm drowning.

"If she keeps pulling me into her room like that, I'm not gonna survive the week."

The voice comes from behind me, casual and amused. I don't turn around. Don't have the energy to pretend I'm okay when Jace's swagger is the last thing I need right now.

"Seriously," he continues, and I hear the soft splash of a stone hitting the fountain. "I mean, don't get me wrong—I'm not complaining. But damn, she's been... intense lately."

Something cold settles in my stomach. The way he says it. Like he's bragging. Like he's grateful.

Like he's getting something I'm not.

Footsteps on gravel, then the stone shifts as he settles beside me. When I finally glance over, he's shirtless, shirt slung over one shoulder, that familiar smug grin on his face.

The grin fades when he sees my expression.

"You okay?"

I don't answer immediately. Can't figure out how to explain that I'm starving in the middle of a feast. That every day I feel more like I'm disappearing.

"I don't think she's feeding me anymore," I say finally.

"What do you mean?"

"I mean I'm hungrier now than I was before I ever touched her."

The words taste bitter. True in a way that makes my chest tight.

Jace goes quiet. Studies my profile in the moonlight with something that might be concern. When he speaks again, his voice has lost its usual edge of humor.

"What can I do?"

The question hits me sideways. Not *what's wrong* or *are you sure* or any of the things I expected. Just—what can I do to help.

Before I can think, before I can second-guess or analyze or talk myself out of it, I grab him by the back of the neck and kiss him.

Hard. Desperate. Like he's air and I've been drowning.

He freezes completely—body going rigid, breath catching against my mouth. For a moment that stretches too long, he doesn't move at all. Just sits there, lips pressed to mine, eyes wide open.

I pull back, immediately regretting it. "Shit. I'm sorry, I—"

But Jace is staring at me, green eyes huge and searching. I can practically see his thoughts racing—confusion, surprise, something that might be want if he'd let himself admit it.

"What the hell was that?" he whispers, but there's no anger in it. Just wonder.

"I don't know," I admit. "I just... I needed it to stop."

"The hunger?"

"The silence."

He blinks, processing. His gaze drops to my mouth, then back to my eyes. I watch him swallow hard, watch something shift in his expression.

Then, slowly—so slowly I almost think I'm imagining it—he leans forward.

This time the kiss is soft. Hesitant. Like he's testing the feel of it, the rightness of it. His hand comes up to cup my jaw, fingers trembling slightly.

When we break apart, we're both breathing hard.

"I keep thinking about the pantry," he says quietly. "About you and Gray. About how watching made me feel."

"How did it make you feel?"

He looks away, color rising in his cheeks. "Like I wanted to be part of it. Which is crazy, because I've never—I don't usually—"

"Hey." I catch his chin gently, turn his face back to mine. "There's no usually here. Just this."

He searches my eyes for a long moment. "You're not gonna hurt me, right?"

The question should sting. Instead, it steadies something inside me. Makes me focus on him instead of the ache.

"Never," I say, and mean it completely. "We go as slow as you want. We stop whenever you want."

He half-laughs, nervous but not pulling away. "I don't think I know what I want."

"That's okay." I shift slightly closer, careful not to crowd him. "We don't have to figure it out right now."

His breathing changes when I lean in to press a soft kiss to his neck. Nothing demanding, just a whisper of contact.

"Is this okay?" I murmur against his skin.

"Yeah," he breathes. "Yeah, it's—fuck, Wes."

I pull back to look at him, watching the way his pupils dilate in the moonlight. His lips are slightly parted, and there's something vulnerable in his expression that makes my chest tight.

"You sure?" I ask quietly. "We can stop here. Just this."

But he shakes his head, reaching up to touch my face with trembling fingers. "I don't want to stop. I just—" He swallows hard. "I don't know what I'm doing."

"Neither do I," I admit. "Not really. We can figure it out together."

Something in his expression shifts—relief, maybe, or recognition that he doesn't have to have all the answers. When I move slowly to straddle his thigh, giving him time to object, he tenses for just a moment before relaxing into it. His hands come up to rest on my waist, tentative but sure.

"Close your eyes," I whisper against the curve of his neck. "If it helps... picture her."

"I don't think I want to." The words come out rough, honest. "I think I just want this. With you."

They hit something deep in my chest that I didn't know was waiting.

"Good."

I slide down slowly, giving him time to process, to object if he wants to. When my knees hit gravel, I look up at him.

"Can I?"

His eyes are dark, pupils dilated, but there's trust there too. He nods, then seems to realize that might not be enough.

"Yeah," he says, voice rough. "Yeah, I want—please."

My hands move to his belt, fingers careful and deliberate. He lifts his hips slightly to help when I work his jeans down just enough. The simple cooperation, the trust in the gesture, makes something warm unfurl in my chest.

One of his hands comes to rest in my hair, not pushing or guiding, just touching. Like he needs the connection as much as I do.

This isn't about taking. It's about giving something real, something that matters. About quieting the gnawing emptiness by focusing entirely on someone else's need.

I start slow, just my mouth against him, tasting salt and warmth. His breathing changes immediately, becomes uneven and sharp. The hand in my hair tightens slightly, and I can feel the tension radiating through his whole body.

"Fuck—Wes—" The words come out broken, desperate.

"I've got you," I murmur against his skin, meaning it in every possible way.

I take him deeper, setting a careful rhythm. He tastes like need and trust, and every soft sound he makes sends heat through my chest. His thighs tremble on either side of me, and I can feel him fighting to stay still, to not overwhelm me.

"It's okay," I whisper, pulling back just enough to speak. "Let go."

When I return to him, using my tongue to trace patterns that make him gasp, his control finally cracks. His hips jerk slightly, and the hand in my hair goes from gentle to desperate.

"I'm close," he warns, voice rough, then lets out a strangled laugh. "Fuck, I feel like a teenager again."

I hum against him in response, doubling my efforts, and feel the exact moment he surrenders completely. His whole body goes taut, back arching off the stone wall as he comes apart with a broken sound that's half my name, half prayer.

The taste of him floods my mouth, and I work him through it until his whole body shudders and the hand in my hair goes gentle, almost reverent.

I rest my forehead against his thigh for a moment, both of us breathing hard.

A memory flashes through me—the first time Bree fed me. That breathless fullness, like every hollow space inside me had been filled with light. The way I felt seen, chosen, complete.

This feels... different. Closer, somehow. Like instead of being filled from the outside, something inside me is finally awake.

Then Jace is sliding down beside me, chest rising and falling in sync with mine. Neither of us speaks for a long moment. The silence doesn't feel empty now—it feels full of something I can't name.

"Still hungry?" he asks finally.

"Less than before."

"Good."

Another pause. Comfortable this time.

"You gonna be okay?"

"No," I say honestly. "But I'm not alone."

Jace gets up slowly, reaches for his discarded shirt. Pulls it over his head with that easy grace of his.

"I should head in."

"Thanks," I say.

He pauses, looking down at me. "For what?"

"For letting me be real with someone."

A small, crooked smile tugs at his lips. The first genuine one I've seen from him all day.

"Anytime." He pauses, shaking his head slightly like he can't quite believe what just happened. But there's no regret in his expression, just wonder. "I mean it. If you need... whatever this was. I'm here." He starts walking toward the sanctuary, then glances back over his shoulder. "Goodnight, Wes."

I watch him go, waiting until his footsteps fade before I turn back to the garden.

The hunger is still there, but muted now. Manageable. Like a constant ache that's finally been acknowledged instead of ignored.

I exhale slowly, letting the night air fill my lungs.

That's when I hear it.

A rustle in the treeline. Soft, deliberate. Not the random movement of wind through leaves.

I go still.

Two glowing eyes blink from the shadows—bright, intelligent, unmistakably wolf. They watch me for a long moment, unblinking and intent.

My pulse spikes.

"Gray?"

No answer. Just those steady, luminous eyes reflecting moonlight.

Then they disappear, melting back into darkness like they were never there at all.

I sit alone in the garden, heart hammering against my ribs, wondering how long he was watching.

Wondering what he saw.

What comes next.

And if he'll ever look at me the same way again.

Chapter 20
RHETT

It's been nearly three weeks since we found her in the chamber.

Standing before that massive mirror, hand pressed to the glass, looking more confident than I'd ever seen her. The mist swirling around her feet was more black than silver, moving with purpose instead of fear. She turned when we called her name and smiled like she'd been waiting for us to find her.

She's been different ever since. Stronger. More certain.

She hasn't slept alone since.

Not because she asked.

Because I couldn't let her.

Sometimes she calls for Jace when I'm already there with her. The old Bree would have asked me to give them privacy, would have been embarrassed about wanting someone else while I was right there.

But now she just pulls Jace into bed with us like it's the most natural thing in the world. When I try to leave—give them space, give myself space to breathe—she tells me to stay.

"I need you both," she says, and her voice carries that new certainty that makes it impossible to argue.

Because the first time I tried to insist, she looked at me like I'd ripped out her heart and stomped on it. So I sit and I watch as she touches him, kisses him, moves with him. My fire magic spikes under my skin—heat that has nowhere to go. Heat crawls up my neck, settles in my chest like a weight I can't shift.

Jace doesn't seem bothered by it—he never has cared much about who's watching. But the way she looks at me while she's with him, making sure I see everything, like my discomfort feeds something in her...

My hands clench against the sheets.

This is what sharing means, right? That jealousy is something I have to work through? She deserves whatever makes her feel whole after everything she's survived.

Maybe she's testing me. Testing how loyal I am, how much I really love her. Making sure I meant it when I said I'd share her with the others.

But sometimes, in the quiet moments, I miss the way she used to flinch when the wind moved the curtains too fast. How she'd curl inward at night, reaching for me like I was her anchor. All those little tells that meant she needed me—they're gone now.

She doesn't startle anymore. Doesn't check over her shoulder for threats. Doesn't grip my hand too tight when we walk past strangers.

I should be happy about that. I am happy. It means she's healing, right? That she finally feels safe.

So why does it feel like I've lost something?

She still reaches for me now, but it's not the same. She doesn't whisper my name in her sleep. Doesn't look at me like she used to when I would touch her cheek. But she still calls me hers.

And gods help me, it's tearing me apart inside.

But I push it down. Like I always do. Like I did when I passed Jace in the hall last night—shirt wrinkled, hair a mess, walking like he'd forgotten where his feet were. He didn't say a word. Just nodded once, eyes wide and dazed, like he'd seen something that rewrote his understanding of the world.

I didn't ask.

There's been a lot of that lately. People not saying what they should. Me not noticing what I don't want to see.

The morning light filters through the sanctuary windows, casting everything in gold. I'm already awake—have been for an hour, just watching her sleep. The way her dark hair spreads across the pillow, the peaceful expression on her face. No nightmares. No terror.

She's safe. Finally, completely safe.

"Morning," she murmurs without opening her eyes, and the sound goes straight through my chest like an arrow.

"Morning, firefly." The nickname slips out naturally now. She never used to let me call her that—too intimate, too presumptuous. Now she melts when I say it.

She stretches against me, all warmth and soft curves, and I have to bite back a groan. Three weeks of this—of her trusting me, choosing me, needing me—and I still can't quite believe it's real.

"Stay with me a little longer?" she asks, and there's something in her voice I can't identify. Not the old hesitation, not fear. Something else. Something that makes my fire magic stir restlessly under my skin.

"As long as you want," I tell her, meaning it completely.

She turns in my arms, green eyes finding mine in the morning light. There's a confidence there that still catches me off guard sometimes. The old Bree would have looked away, would have doubted her right to ask for what she wanted.

But now she knows she's wanted. Knows she's mine to protect.

"Will you make tea?" she asks, fingers tracing patterns on my chest. "That blend Theo brought back from the market?"

"Of course."

She rewards me with a smile that could power the sanctuary for a week. "You're so good to me."

The words do something to me every time she says them. Good to her. Like it's a choice, like I could be anything else. Like I wasn't built specifically for this—to shield her from harm, to anticipate her needs, to be the wall between her and everything that wants to hurt her.

I press a kiss to her forehead, breathing in vanilla and something deeper, something that makes my magic purr with contentment.

"Always," I promise.

The kitchen is quiet when I pad downstairs, bare feet silent on cool stone. Most of the sanctuary is still sleeping—these early hours have become sacred to me. Time when it's just us, just the soft sounds of her breathing and the steady beat of my heart against her back.

I measure out the tea carefully. Earl grey with bergamot, and a touch of honey. The way she's started taking it lately. Not the simple chamomile she used to prefer, but something richer, more complex. At least that's what Theo tells me.

She's changing. Growing. Becoming the woman she was always meant to be.

The water is just reaching a boil when arms slip around my waist from behind. Familiar weight, familiar warmth. She presses a kiss between my shoulder blades, and heat flares through me so suddenly I have to grip the counter to stay upright.

"Smells perfect," she murmurs against my skin.

"Not ready yet," I manage, though my voice comes out rougher than intended.

"I wasn't talking about the tea."

Her hands slide under my shirt, palms flat against my stomach, and my fire magic responds like she's struck a match. Heat races through my veins, pooling under my skin wherever she touches.

She laughs softly, a sound I'm still getting used to. Rich and knowing and completely unafraid.

"I love how you react to me," she says, lips moving against my spine. Her hands drift lower, fingers working at my belt. "Like you can't help yourself."

I can't. That's the truth of it. My breath catches as her hand slips inside my pants, warm fingers wrapping around me with confident familiarity.

"The others are worried about you," she says, voice conversational even as her hand moves with deliberate slowness.

I try to focus on her words, but heat is building under my skin, making it hard to think. "What do you mean?"

"Gray asked me yesterday if you were okay." Her thumb traces over the head of my cock, and I have to grip the counter to stay upright. "Said you've been... intense lately."

My hips jerk into her touch before I can stop myself. "Are you—fuck—are you worried about me?"

She increases her pace slightly, and my vision blurs at the edges. "No. I like you intense. I like that you can't bear to let me out of your sight."

The kettle whistles, but I can barely hear it over the blood rushing in my ears. Her free hand reaches around me to turn off the burner while she continues stroking me with maddening precision.

"I can't lose you again," I manage, the words torn from somewhere deep in my chest. "After we found you in that chamber—"

"Shh." Her teeth graze my shoulder blade, and I'm lost. "You didn't lose me. I'm right here."

Her hand moves faster, and the fire under my skin flares brighter. For just a moment, I swear I feel something pull from me—warmth, energy, something essential. But then I'm coming apart in her hands, pleasure washing over me in waves, and rational thought disappears entirely.

"I'm not going anywhere," she whispers against my spine as I shake in her arms. "I promise."

I believe her. Gods help me, with her touch still burning on my skin, I believe everything she tells me.

Even when a voice in the back of my head whispers that promises can be broken. That the woman we found standing at that mirror, confident and unafraid, felt different than the one who used to reach for me in the dark.

Even when I remember how she used to take her tea with just honey, no bergamot.

Even when my fire magic reacts to her touch like it's trying to tell me something I'm not ready to hear.

But Bree deserves whatever makes her feel whole. Whatever helps her heal. If that means enduring the performance, the tests, the way she looks at me while she's with Jace—then that's what I'll do.

She's been through too much to have me questioning her now. Too much pain, too much fear. If this is who she needs to be to feel safe, to feel powerful, then I'll be whatever she needs me to be.

Even if it's tearing me apart.

Even if some nights I lie awake missing the girl who used to flinch at shadows and reach for me like I was the only solid thing in her world.

This is what love means, right? Putting her needs first. Protecting her from everything that wants to hurt her.

Even protecting her from my own doubts.

Chapter 21
GRAY

Sleep won't come.

I've been staring at the ceiling for hours, replaying what I saw in the garden last night. Jace and Wes. The way Wes dropped to his knees, desperate and hungry and real. The sound Jace made when he came apart, the careful way Wes worked him through it.

I press the heels of my hands against my closed eyes, but the images won't fade. The memory sits heavy in my chest—not jealousy, exactly. Something more complicated. Something that makes my skin feel too tight and my pulse kick up every time I think about how long I stood there watching.

How much I wanted to step out of the shadows.

The pre-dawn air in my room feels suffocating. I need to move, need space to think without the weight of these walls pressing down on me.

My bare feet are silent on the cold stone floors as I head toward the kitchen. Maybe I'll make tea. Maybe I'll just sit and try to sort through what I'm feeling without anyone else watching me do it.

That's when I hear it.

Rhett's voice, rough and desperate: "I can't lose you again."

I freeze at the kitchen doorway.

Bree is pressed against Rhett's back, her hand moving rhythmically inside his unbuttoned jeans. His hips rock into her touch, head thrown back, completely lost in what she's doing to him.

Her eyes are calm. Predatory. Like she's studying his reactions instead of sharing them.

That's not the shy, overwhelmed girl who used to blush when we so much as held her hand too long.

Rhett shudders as he comes, and she whispers something against his spine that makes him go boneless. When she pulls her hand free, she catches sight of me standing in the shadows.

Our eyes meet.

She doesn't look embarrassed. Doesn't look caught.

She smiles.

"Gray." Her voice is warm honey, like finding me watching was exactly what she hoped for. "Couldn't sleep either?"

Jace would lose his damn mind if he walked in on this.

The thought hits me out of nowhere, sharp and defensive and completely irrelevant to the situation. But it grounds me somehow. Gives me something to focus on besides the way she's looking at me like I'm her next meal.

Rhett's still catching his breath, but he turns to face us both, tucking himself back into his pants. His fire magic is settling under his skin, satisfied and warm. He looks at Bree like she just gave him everything he's ever wanted.

She steps away from him and walks toward me, still wearing that serene smile. Her hand—the same one that was just wrapped around Rhett—reaches for my chest.

I sidestep before she can touch me.

"I was just—" I clear my throat, backing toward the door. "Needed some air. Gonna run the perimeter."

"Gray, wait—" Rhett starts, but I'm already turning away.

"It's fine," I say without looking back. "Just needed to clear my head."

I leave them standing there—Rhett confused and sated, Bree watching me with those too-calm eyes.

As I reach the hallway, one thought cuts through everything else, sharp and certain:

That wasn't Bree.

The realization settles cold and heavy in my chest, and something wild and desperate claws at my ribs. I need to move. Need to run. Need to get as far away from that wrongness as possible before it chokes me.

I walk quickly through the kitchen, past the lingering scent of what just happened, and slip out the back door into the garden. The pre-dawn air hits my skin, and I don't make it more than a few steps before the shift takes me.

The change comes easier now than it did in the beginning—bones stretching and realigning without the sharp agony I remember from those first times. White fur ripples along my limbs as I drop to four legs, and suddenly the world explodes into scents and sounds that make everything clearer. I run through the garden and into the forest beyond, paws hitting soft earth and fallen leaves as I follow instincts that lead me exactly where I need to go.

The chamber.

The chamber calls to me like a wound that won't heal.

I find myself at the top of the stairs without consciously deciding to come here. The space feels different than it did that morning we found Bree standing at the mirror.

"This fucking chamber," I breathe as I head down the stairs.

As I reach the bottom, I see it—the mirror stands against the far wall, the mirror Bree was touching. Its surface reflects nothing but darkness.

As I approach it, I expect to see my reflection, but instead there's nothing but black.

Weird.

All the ash piles are gone. Every trace of the failed attempts, the broken dreams, the people who reached for something and found only death—erased like they never existed.

Weeks ago, this place was a graveyard. Now it looks like it's been waiting.

The temperature drops immediately, cold seeping through my skin and settling in my bones. My breath fogs in the suddenly frigid air, and something deep in my chest responds to the change—something that's been stirring ever since Bree touched the crown.

The mirror's surface ripples like disturbed water. I'm still standing directly in front of it, close enough to see my own reflection staring back. But there's something else there too. Something moving behind my image, dark and indistinct.

That's when I hear it, a murmur. Desperate. Coming from somewhere else in the chamber.

I follow the sound, moving carefully around the outer edge of the circular space. The voice grows clearer as I get closer—a woman's voice, frantic with desperation.

"I can't—why can't I—where's my other half?"

I find her on the far side of the chamber, pressed against one of the mirrors with both palms flat against the glass. She's maybe forty, dressed in traveling clothes that look like she's been on the road for days. Her dark hair is disheveled, and there's a wild edge to her movements.

"They said it was open again," she mutters, pressing harder against the mirror. "That the Ether restored the Oath. Where are you?"

"Hey," I say quietly, not wanting to startle her. "Are you okay?"

She whirls around, eyes wide and desperate. "You can see me? You're real?"

"Yeah, I'm real." I take a careful step closer. "What are you trying to do?"

"The Oath," she says, turning back to the mirror. "I felt it awaken. Felt the pull all the way from the mountains. My other half is supposed to be here. She's supposed to answer."

Footsteps echo from another part of the chamber. A man emerges from the shadows between two mirrors, and everything about him radiates power. His movements are too fluid, too controlled, and for just a second his eyes flash with an inner light—silver and predatory.

When he smiles, I catch the flash of fangs.

Vampire.

"Still trying, I see," he says to the woman, his voice calm and almost gentle. He places a hand on her shoulder, and she seems to relax slightly under his touch.

"Put your hand on the mirror," he suggests. "Sometimes it takes time for the connection to form."

She presses her palm against the glass again, hope flickering in her expression. But nothing happens. The mirror remains just a mirror, showing only her own reflection.

The vampire turns to me, studying my face with those predatory eyes. "You're one of hers."

"Yeah."

He nods knowingly, turning back to the woman. "Hybrid," he says gently, like he's stating a simple fact about the weather. "That's why it's not working. You're already whole, you see. Two halves in one body."

The woman lets out a broken sob, her hand sliding down the mirror's surface. "But I felt the pull. I felt it calling to me."

"Your Feeder half," the vampire explains, still gentle. "It recognizes the hunger, the incompleteness others feel. But the Oath can't give you what you already have."

"She's not coming," the woman whispers. "She's never coming."

"Because she doesn't exist," he says softly. "The mirror realm sees you as complete. There's no other half to call."

I watch him guide the woman away from the mirror, his movements careful and kind. But there's something in his eyes—satisfaction, maybe. Like he expected this outcome.

As they disappear into the shadows, I'm left alone with the mirrors.

Walking back through the chamber, my eyes catch on one mirror I hadn't noticed before. The frame is carved with intricate wolf heads, their eyes seeming to follow my movement. Something about it draws me forward, a pull I can't quite explain.

I stop directly in front of it.

The surface flickers—just once—like a candle flame disturbed by breath.

My reflection stares back at me, but there's something different about it. Something in the eyes that doesn't quite match what I'm feeling.

My hand rises toward the glass before I can stop myself.

The moment my palm touches the surface, my reflection changes.

It smirks.

Not me. Not my expression. But something wearing my face, looking back at me with knowledge I don't possess and confidence I've never felt.

The reflection tilts its head, and I feel the pull—sharp and desperate, like hunger that's gone too long unfed. It wants me to stay. To keep touching the glass. To let it show me what I could be.

I jerk my hand back, but every instinct I have screams at me to reach out again.

No.

I force myself to turn away, to walk toward the stairs, even though it feels like tearing something vital out of my chest.

Behind me, I swear I can feel it watching. Waiting for me to change my mind.

And I know—with terrible certainty—that I will.

Chapter 22
THANE

The children are playing in the garden when I find them.

Three of them—refugees from the northern territories, barely old enough to understand why their parents brought them here. They've built a fort out of fallen branches beneath the mira trees, their laughter echoing off the sanctuary walls like something precious and fragile.

The youngest one, a girl with dark curls, looks up as I approach. Her eyes go wide—not with fear, exactly, but with the careful awareness children learn when they've seen too much too young.

"Is everything okay?" she asks.

The question hits harder than it should. Because no, everything is not okay. The woman these children think saved them hasn't walked these paths in weeks. Hasn't checked on the crops, or asked about the barriers, or stopped to watch them play the way she used to.

I know why she stopped.

But they don't.

"Everything's fine," I tell her, crouching down to her level. "Just making sure everyone's settled."

She studies my face with the intensity only children possess. "You're not her."

"No," I agree. "I'm not."

"Will she come back?"

The question lodges in my throat like broken glass. Because the real answer—that she never left, but something else is wearing her face—isn't something I can explain to a six-year-old who's already lost everything once.

"I don't know," I say instead. "But you're safe here. I promise."

She nods solemnly, then returns to her game. But I catch the way her shoulders stay tense, the way she glances toward the sanctuary doors like she's waiting for someone who might never come.

She'll walk this path again if I have anything to say about it. I will find her.

I straighten and continue my rounds.

This is what Bree used to do. Every morning, without fail. Check the perimeter. Visit the newest arrivals. Make sure the children were eating, the elderly were comfortable, the Feeders weren't pushing themselves too hard. Small gestures that kept the sanctuary functioning as more than just a collection of refugees hiding from the world.

I'm efficient at it. Thorough. But I lack her warmth, the way she made everyone feel seen instead of managed.

Still, it needs doing. And if she's not, if this impostor won't, then someone has to fill the void.

The irony isn't lost on me. For centuries, I served the Council's interests above everything else. Played their game, followed their rules, convinced myself that survival required sacrificing pieces of my soul until nothing remained but strategy and hunger.

Now I find myself protecting the very thing they want to destroy.

A woman walks toward me from the eastern garden—Mairen, the Feeder woman who arrived first with her family. Her face brightens when she sees me, relief evident in the way her shoulders relax.

"Thane," she says, slightly breathless. "I was hoping to catch you. The children have been asking about magic lessons. Nothing dangerous," she adds quickly. "Just... basics. How to recognize their gifts when they emerge."

The request is reasonable. Necessary, even. Most of the refugee children have magical parents but no formal training. They'll need guidance as their abilities develop.

But the thought of organizing lessons, of planning for their futures, assumes we have a future to plan for.

"I'll see what can be arranged," I tell her. "Perhaps Theo could help. His gift is gentle enough for children."

"Thank you." Her smile is genuine, grateful. "It would mean so much to them. To all of us."

I nod and turn to continue my rounds, but her voice stops me.

"Thane?" She hesitates, then forges ahead. "Is she... is everything all right with her?"

The question I've been dreading.

"What do you mean?"

"She seems different lately. Distant. I know she has responsibilities, but..." Mairen wraps her arms around herself. "She used to stop and talk. Ask about the children by name. Now she barely acknowledges us when she passes through."

My jaw tightens. Because Mairen is right. The woman wearing Bree's face—because that's who we're really discussing—treats the refugees like subjects instead of people. Useful when they serve her purposes, invisible when they don't.

"She's been under a great deal of pressure," I say carefully. "Leading isn't easy."

"Of course not." But doubt lingers in Mairen's expression. "It's just... when she first came to us, it felt like she understood. Like she'd been where we were. Now it feels like she's already forgotten."

Pain flares beneath my ribs, sudden and searing.

The summons burns through my flesh like acid, and I barely manage to keep my expression neutral as the Council's brand activates beneath my skin. Not now. Not when I'm finally starting to understand the full scope of what this deception is costing these people.

"I'm sorry," I manage, pressing a hand to my side. "Council business. I'll be back."

Mairen's face immediately shifts to concern. "Are you all right?"

"Fine." The word comes out sharper than intended. "Just... duty calls."

I turn and walk quickly toward the sanctuary, needing to be away from witnesses before the magic takes hold. Behind me, I hear Mairen calling out something about hoping everything goes well, but her voice fades as the summons intensifies.

The magic wraps around me like chains, pulling me sideways through space. Light and shadow twist into a corridor of sound, disorienting and nauseating, until—

The Chamber of Five materializes around me.

Same black throne, same position of deliberate inferiority. But this time, the atmosphere is different from our last meeting. Where before there was agitation and threats, now there's something that might be satisfaction.

Valdris paces near her throne, but her flames dance with controlled pleasure rather than agitation. Nyx looks more relaxed than I've seen her in months, draped across her throne with the lazy contentment of a predator whose hunt has succeeded.

Even Marcus seems less rigid than usual, his steel throne reflecting what might be approval.

Only Eris maintains her typical distant expression, silver eyes unfocused as she stares at something none of us can see.

"Thane," Valdris says as I take my seat. "Your timing is impeccable."

I settle into my black stone throne and wait. The shift from our last meeting—when they were ready to unleash Phil immediately—to this is jarring.

"We have an update," Marcus announces. "A change in strategy."

"Phil's visit didn't go as planned," Valdris admits with obvious irritation. "His methods proved... less effective than anticipated."

My blood runs cold, but I keep my expression neutral. "I'm not surprised."

"However," Nyx continues smoothly, "her influence continues to grow. More refugees arrive daily. Her following expands."

"Which brings us to our decision," Marcus says. "The Council has voted."

Here it comes.

"The Ashen Oath will be reopened," Valdris announces. "Effective immediately."

The words hit me like ice, but I force myself to remain still. "I see."

"Under proper oversight, naturally," Nyx adds, her smile never wavering.

"What sort of oversight?" I ask carefully.

"We'll need access to the chamber she unlocked," Marcus explains. "Full access. No restrictions."

"And in exchange," Valdris continues with obvious satisfaction, "we're prepared to consider offering her a sixth seat. Full Council membership, assuming everything proceeds smoothly."

A trap disguised as an honor. Give us what we want first, and maybe we'll reward you later.

"Elementals and Seers will have unrestricted access," Marcus counts off. "Shifters as well, provided they demonstrate adequate control. Mentalists require pre-approval—standard for advanced magical workings."

He pauses, and I know what's coming.

"Feeders, however, will be prohibited entirely."

The world tilts.

"Prohibited?" I keep my voice level.

"Completely," Valdris confirms. "The research is clear—Feeder participation creates dangerous imbalances. Too much potential for exploitation."

"Those who attempt unauthorized participation," Marcus continues with clinical precision, "will face binding. Magic stripped, feeding capabilities severed."

Binding. Slow starvation. Death.

"You're condemning them," I say quietly.

"We're protecting the magical community," Marcus corrects. "Feeders have always struggled with control. This removes the temptation."

"How thoughtful," I murmur.

Valdris's flames flicker higher. "We knew you'd understand. After all, you've been monitoring her progress. You know better than anyone how dangerous unchecked power can be."

"The growing refugee population at her sanctuary," Nyx adds with pointed emphasis, "demonstrates her influence continues to expand. Better to work with that reality than against it."

The pragmatism of it sits in my stomach like poison.

Because that's exactly what the imposter has given them over the last few weeks. Compliance disguised as strength. A Source who plays by their rules instead of challenging their authority.

Everything Bree would never have accepted.

"When does this take effect?" I ask.

"Once we've inspected the chamber and confirmed access," Marcus says. "The announcement will be made after we've verified everything is in working order."

"How thoughtful," I murmur.

The timeline gives me something to work with. Not much, but something.

"Phil has been exceedingly pleased with the progress," Nyx adds with a razor smile. "Especially since that incident at the sanctuary. He says she's been far more... cooperative since then."

My stomach clenches. Phil reporting back on Bree's behavior. Watching. Evaluating. It's disgusting.

"Cooperative," I repeat carefully.

"Precisely," Marcus says with satisfaction. "No more erratic outbursts. No more dangerous surges. She's learned to channel her power appropriately."

"There is one more thing," Eris says suddenly, her voice hollow and distant. All conversation stops. When the Seer speaks during Council meetings, we listen.

"Change comes," she continues, silver eyes unfocused. "Not the change we planned. Not the change we seek. The girl... there are two paths before her. One leads to the throne we would build. The other..."

She trails off, blinking slowly.

"The other?" Valdris prompts.

"The other leads nowhere we can follow." Eris's gaze suddenly sharpens, focusing directly on me. "Choose carefully, Feeder. The future turns on choices not yet made."

A chill runs down my spine. Seers rarely speak directly to individual Council members, and never in riddles this pointed.

"I'm sure I don't know what you mean," I say.

"Don't you?" Her smile is slight, knowing. "I think you know exactly what I mean."

The meeting concludes with typical Council efficiency—assignments distributed, timelines established, responsibilities clarified. I sit through it all with perfect composure, playing the role they expect.

But inside, I'm calculating.

The Oath is open, but poisoned. The Council thinks they have their perfect compliant Source. And somewhere in the sanctuary, refugees will soon celebrating news that will ultimately destroy them.

All because they're trusting a woman who isn't the person they think she is.

As the others begin to disperse, Valdris catches my attention.

"Tell your queen we're grateful for her obedience," she says with a smile that suggests she knows exactly how that word will land.

Obedience.

I don't answer. Just nod once and let the Council magic pull me back to the sanctuary.

But as I materialize in the garden where I started, one thought echoes through my mind with terrible clarity:

Bree would never have been obedient.

Which means I'm running out of time to save her.

Chapter 23
JACE

The firelight flickers across her skin like liquid gold.

I'm between her thighs, lost in the taste of her, the way she moves beneath my mouth. Her fingers are tangled in my hair, holding me exactly where she wants me, and fuck—I love this version of her. Confident. Demanding. No hesitation, no apologies.

"Don't stop," she breathes, and the command sends heat straight through me.

I wasn't planning to. Haven't been able to think about anything else for hours except making her feel good, making her forget everything except this moment. The way she says my name when I find the right spot, the way her thighs tighten around my shoulders when she's close.

She's different now. Stronger. More willing to take what she wants instead of waiting for permission. It started after that morning we found her in the chamber alone. Like something inside her finally clicked into place. The hesitation that used to make her flinch away from touch, from pleasure, from us—it's gone. Replaced by something that makes my pulse race every time she looks at me.

The old Bree would have blushed at half the things she whispers in my ear now. Would have hidden under covers instead of sprawling across her bed like she owns the world.

This Bree? This Bree takes what she wants and makes no apologies for it.

I fucking love it.

My tongue finds that spot that makes her arch beneath me, and her grip in my hair tightens. "There," she gasps. "Right there."

The authority in her voice makes me want to do whatever it takes to keep hearing it. I've always been good at reading people, at finding what makes them laugh or squirm or lose control. But with her, it's become an obsession. Every sound, every tremor, every breathless command.

The knock at the door makes me freeze mid-motion.

Any normal person would call out "just a minute" or tell whoever it is to go away. Any normal person would be mortified at the interruption.

"Come in," she says instead, barely breathless, like having someone walk in on us is the most natural thing in the world.

Um...

I lift my head slightly, disbelief coursing through me, but she presses me back down with a firm hand. Her palm is warm against my scalp, possessive.

"I said don't stop."

What the fuck?

The door opens. Footsteps. A pause that stretches too long.

My heart is hammering against my ribs, but not entirely from embarrassment. There's something thrilling about this—about being claimed so completely that she doesn't care who sees. About being hers in a way that's undeniable.

"We need to talk." Thane's voice, clipped and professional.

I can't see him from this angle, but I can feel the tension shift in the room. The weight of his presence. Bree doesn't even flinch.

"Then talk," she says simply.

My brain short-circuits. She wants me to keep going? With Thane standing right there?

But her hand is still in my hair, stroking through the strands like I'm exactly where I belong, makes the decision for me. If she's not embarrassed, then neither am I.

I press my mouth back to her, feel her respond immediately. Her breathing picks up again, and I have to bite back a groan at how perfectly she fits against my tongue.

"They've requested to visit the sanctuary," Thane says, his voice carefully neutral. "The Council. Two weeks from now. A formal dinner, followed by an inspection of the chamber."

The words filter through the haze of heat and want, but it's hard to concentrate when Bree's fingers are stroking through my hair and her thighs are trembling on either side of my head.

Council visit. Inspection. Those should be alarming words, but right now all I can think about is the way she tastes and the soft sounds she's making.

"Tell them they're welcome," she responds, calm and collected like she's discussing the weather instead of hosting the people who've been trying to control her for months, while I work between her legs. "We'll prepare a proper reception."

"What kind of inspection?" I manage to ask, lifting my head slightly so I can see her face.

"The Ashen Oath chamber," Thane answers. "They want to see it. Verify access."

Bree's hand tightens in my hair, not in pleasure but in something sharper. There's a flicker of something in her eyes—calculation, maybe. Planning.

"Perfect," she says, and I can see the way her lips curve into a smile that doesn't quite reach her eyes. "It's time they saw what real power looks like."

I press a soft kiss to the inside of her thigh, keeping my mouth busy while watching her face. There's a pause. Something unspoken passing between her and Thane, and even though I can see her expression, I can't read the full dynamic between them. The air feels charged in a way that has nothing to do with what we were doing before he arrived.

"You can go now, Thane," she says, and there's an edge to her voice that wasn't there before. Not cruel, exactly, but dismissive. Final. "Unless there's something else?"

Another pause. Longer this time.

"Two weeks, then." His footsteps retreat. The door closes with a soft click.

The moment he's gone, the tension in Bree's body shifts back to something purely physical. She exhales slowly, like nothing unusual just happened.

"Where were we?"

I look up at her, half-dazed by the whiplash between political maneuvering and this. "You want me to—"

"Finish."

The command in her voice, the way the firelight catches in her eyes and turns them molten—it's intoxicating. I dive back in with renewed focus, the adrenaline from being watched somehow making everything more intense.

She's close now, I can tell from the way her breathing changes, the way her fingers clench and release in my hair. I work her with single-minded determination, chasing every gasp and tremor until she breaks apart beneath my mouth.

When she comes, her hand knots tight in my hair, and I feel the tremor that runs through her entire body. The soft gasp that escapes her lips, my name falling from her mouth like a prayer.

I stay there for a moment, pressing gentle kisses to her inner thigh, savoring the way she shivers at the contact. When I finally look up, she's watching me with a satisfied smile that makes my chest tight with something that might be love or might be worship. Maybe both.

"I love it when you're bossy," I say, grinning up at her.

She laughs softly, the sound rich and satisfied. "Then you'll love me even more by the time the Council arrives."

Something about the way she says it makes my stomach flutter—not with excitement, but with something like unease. Like there's meaning layered beneath the words that I'm missing.

But then she's pulling me up to kiss her, and whatever I felt dissolves under the press of her mouth against mine.

I eventually slip out of bed, pulling my shirt back on and trying to shake off the post-sex haze. My body feels loose and satisfied, but my mind is spinning from what just happened. Not just the sex—though that was incredible—but the whole thing. The way she handled Thane's interruption like it was nothing. The casual way she dismissed him. The authority in her voice when she talked about the Council.

When did she become so… commanding?

The kitchen seems like a good idea—water, maybe something to eat, something to ground myself back in reality. The sanctuary is quiet at this hour, most people asleep, but there's always someone awake. Night shift rotations, insomniacs, people with nightmares.

I'm halfway down the hall when I nearly collide with Wes coming around the corner.

"Shit, sorry—" I start, then stop when I get a good look at him.

His hair is disheveled, shirt wrinkled like he threw it on in a hurry. There's something different about his face too—a looseness around his eyes, like tension that's finally been released. And he smells like…

Oh.

The realization hits me like a freight train, and suddenly I'm very aware of how I must look. Hair messed up from her fingers, lips probably still swollen, the faint scent of her perfume clinging to my clothes.

We stare at each other for a beat too long.

"Late night?" Wes asks, and there's something almost amused in his voice.

"Yeah, you could say that." I clear my throat, feeling heat creep up my neck. "You too, apparently."

His mouth quirks up at one corner. "Something like that."

We're both trying so hard to be casual about this, but there's no hiding what we've both been doing. The evidence is written all over us—the satisfied exhaustion, the lingering flush, the way we're both avoiding direct eye contact.

"So…" I trail off, not sure what the protocol is here. Do we compare notes? Pretend this isn't awkward as hell? Make jokes about sharing?

"She's different lately," Wes says quietly, and there's something careful in his tone. "More... confident."

"Yeah." I nod maybe too eagerly. "She knows what she wants now. It's incredible."

"Incredible," Wes echoes, but there's a flicker of something in his expression I can't read.

"I mean, she used to be so hesitant about everything," I continue, because talking feels better than standing here in loaded silence. "Now she just takes what she wants. It's like she finally stepped into who she's supposed to be."

Wes nods slowly. "Right. Who she's supposed to be."

There's something in the way he says it that makes me pause. Like he's testing the words, seeing how they taste.

"You okay?" I ask.

"Fine." He runs a hand through his already-messed hair. "Just... tired."

"Right. Well." I gesture vaguely toward the kitchen. "I was just going to grab some water. You want anything?"

"I'm good. Thanks though."

We stand there for another awkward moment, the weight of what we're not talking about pressing down between us.

"I should..." Wes gestures toward his room.

"Yeah. Me too."

But neither of us moves.

"Jace?" Wes's voice is quiet, almost uncertain.

"Yeah?"

For a second, it looks like he's going to say something important. Something that might cut through all the careful politeness and get to whatever's really bothering him.

Instead, he steps closer and kisses me.

It's soft, brief—nothing like the desperate hunger from before. Just his lips against mine for a heartbeat, warm and sure.

When he pulls back, his eyes are serious. "This doesn't change anything. What happened between us."

My chest tightens. "Wes—"

"Goodnight, Jace."

He's already moving before I can figure out what to say back.

I watch him walk away, noting the tension in his shoulders that wasn't there before. The way he keeps glancing back toward Bree's room like he's forgotten something but can't remember what.

When I finally make it to the kitchen, I can't shake the feeling that there was more to that conversation and that kiss than either of us was willing to admit. Something lurking underneath the surface awkwardness that felt heavier than simple post-sex weirdness.

But as I drink my water and head back to my own room, Bree's satisfied smile fills my mind and pushes everything else aside.

She's finally becoming who she's meant to be. And whatever small doubts might be creeping around the edges, they're not worth examining too closely.

Not when she's finally, truly happy.

Chapter 24
STELLAN

The sanctuary kitchen at breakfast is a study in practiced normalcy.

Jace stands at the stove, flipping pancakes with more focus than the task requires, hair still sticking up on one side from sleep. The smell of butter and coffee fills the air, mixing with the sound of scraping plates and muffled conversation. Rhett sits at the counter, close enough to steal bites when Jace isn't looking. Wes stares out the window like he's seeing something the rest of us can't.

Theo has a folded piece of paper beside his plate—correspondence from somewhere, judging by the careful way he's not looking at it. Gray sits at the far end of the table, silent and watchful, picking at food he's not really eating. Thane occupies his usual spot near the wall, silver eyes tracking every movement with predatory focus.

All of them here. All of them avoiding what matters.

It's been three days since Thane told me about the Council's decision. Three days since I went to Zira, knowing she'd feel the need to protect Feeders as much as I did. Three days since we've been working around the clock to get as many through the Oath as possible before the hammer falls.

And three days of watching the woman wearing Bree's face plan this Council dinner like it's her sixteenth birthday party instead of a political execution.

"You're gonna burn those," Rhett mumbles, nodding toward the stove.

"I don't burn things," Jace says without turning around. "I create controlled breakfast experiences."

"Is that what we're calling it now?" Wes's mouth quirks up slightly. "Because I remember some very uncontrolled heat experiences lately."

"Shut up." But Jace is grinning, and for a moment, they almost look like the same boys who stumbled into this place months ago.

The illusion doesn't last.

"Anyone know what the hell is up with Bree lately?"

Zira's voice cuts through the kitchen chatter like a blade. She stands in the doorway, dark curls wild from the morning wind, eyes sharp with the kind of focused irritation that means someone's about to get uncomfortable.

Every fork stops midair. The easy banter dies.

Jace nearly drops a pancake. "What—what do you mean?"

Zira rolls her eyes and stalks to the counter, helping herself to a mug like she owns the place. "Don't play dumb. The Council's coming in less than two weeks, and she's acting like it's a fucking holiday instead of the end of the world."

Rhett's shoulders tense immediately. "She's handling it."

"If by 'handling it' you mean spending yesterday afternoon debating whether the napkins should be silver or pearl, then sure." Zira pours coffee with sharp, precise movements. "She's handling it perfectly."

"She's been different since the chamber," Theo offers carefully, diplomatic as always. "But maybe she's still adjusting to—"

"Adjusting?" Zira's laugh has no humor in it. "She spent three hours yesterday discussing floral arrangements. For the people coming to kill us. She's not Bree anymore."

The silence that follows is suffocating. Even the morning light streaming through the windows seems dimmer, like the words have weight enough to push back against the sun.

I set down my mug with deliberate care. "Enough."

Zira turns that sharp gaze on me, but there's understanding there. We've had this conversation already, in private. This performance is for their benefit.

"Walk with me," I say quietly.

Zira hesitates for the appropriate beat, then follows me toward the back door. Behind us, the boys sit in heavy quiet, pretending they can't feel the foundation of their world shifting beneath their feet.

The garden air is cool against my skin, a relief after the stifling tension of the kitchen. Birds call from the mira trees, and somewhere in the distance, I can hear the soft hum of the sanctuary's wards—magic woven so deeply into the stone it's become part of the architecture.

We walk toward the chamber path without speaking. The performance is over now; we can speak freely.

When I went to Zira three nights ago, I knew she'd understand immediately. She's seen enough of the magical world's politics to recognize when something is wrong, and she cares about Feeders in a way that makes her dangerous to those who would harm us. Thane's revelation about the Council's ban made her the perfect ally.

"The latest count?" I ask as we move out of earshot.

"Forty-three since we started," she reports, voice low and efficient. "Thanks to you and Thane keeping her distracted, we've been able to bring them through after dark. The word is spreading faster than we expected."

"Good. How many are staying?"

"About half. The others take the Oath and leave, but they're stronger now. Different." She glances at me. "They'll remember this when the time comes."

I pause, considering. "We need to move on the others soon. Get them through before the ban takes effect."

"The guys?"

"Wes and Thane, specifically. Any Feeders who haven't taken the Oath yet." I keep my voice low, even though we're well away from the sanctuary now. "Once the Council ban goes into effect, it won't matter what she says. They'll strip magic from anyone who tries."

"And the others? The non-Feeders?"

"They should be fine. The ban only applies to Feeders." I consider the timeline. "But Wes and Thane need to go through tonight. Before the Council realizes how many we've already gotten through."

Zira nods, then fixes me with a sharp look. "You should too."

I don't argue. She's right.

"What about all of them though?" she continues. "Bree's guys. If they all take the Oath, become stronger... the Council might see that as too much power gathered in one place. Too much threat."

"Perhaps." I consider this. "But scattered power is weak power. And if we're right about what's happened to Bree, we'll need every advantage we can get when the truth comes out. Better her people are strong enough to fight back."

"You think it'll come to that?"

"I think," I say carefully, "that we should be prepared for any possibility."

We continue toward the chamber, where the air grows thick with magic. The Ashen Oath has been working overtime these past few days, responding to every Feeder who approaches it with desperate hunger.

"She's going to notice soon," Zira says, though we both know this isn't true. "You can't keep sneaking people in forever."

"We're not sneaking." I keep my voice soft, but there's steel underneath. "We're reclaiming what's ours. She's too busy planning party favors to look beneath her own feet."

It still amazes me how completely she's dismissed the magical activity happening under her nose. The real Bree would have known something was going on. Would have been there to welcome them, to understand what they needed.

This version is so focused on her Council performance that she's blind to everything else.

"Forty-three Feeders stronger than they were less than a week ago," Zira muses. "And more coming every night. When the Council arrives expecting to find broken refugees..."

"They'll find an army instead." The satisfaction in my voice is real. "One they never saw coming."

We reach the clearing just before the chamber entrance. The air here pulses with energy—silver and black threads weaving visibly through the morning light. Beautiful and wrong at the same time.

"It's stronger every night," Zira observes.

I reach out to touch the carved doorframe, fingers tracing symbols that pulse faintly under my skin. The chamber recognizes me now, accepts my presence. But there's something else underneath—a deep, ancient wrongness that makes my teeth ache.

"The Oath is alive again," I murmur. "You can feel it, can't you?"

She nods, awe and fear mixing in her dark eyes.

"It remembers who it belongs to." The words taste bitter. "Which makes this even more dangerous. Because I don't think the right person is wearing the crown."

"You mean whoever that is isn't really Bree?"

"Exactly." I turn to face her fully. "The chamber doesn't care about our politics or our hierarchies. It knows what it was built for, and it knows who has the right to command it. And right now..."

"Right now it's responding to someone who might not be her." Zira's voice drops to a whisper.

Understanding dawns in her expression, followed quickly by alarm. "Then why is it answering for us?"

"Because it's finally awake again." The admission carries weight. "It's been waiting for the Scarborne line to reopen it, and now that it has... now that Bree has, the chamber is functioning as it was meant to. Any true magical being can access the Oath now that the seal is broken."

"But for how long?"

"That's the question, isn't it?" I meet her eyes. "The chamber belongs to Scarborne blood. If something happens to the real Bree, if that bloodline is compromised..."

"The Oath could close again."

"Or worse. It could turn against those it deems unworthy." I touch the doorframe again, feeling that wrongness pulse beneath the ancient power. "We need to move quickly."

Zira studies me with those sharp, knowing eyes. "What are you going to do?"

"What I always do." The answer comes easily. "Balance the scales before someone decides to tip them for good."

She tilts her head. "You think Thane's ready for that fight?"

I allow myself a small smile. "Thane's already fighting it. He just hasn't realized it yet."

We stand in comfortable silence for a moment, listening to the chamber hum beneath our feet. The sound is hypnotic—like a heartbeat, like breathing, like something vast and patient waiting to wake up fully.

"Two weeks," Zira says quietly. "The Council's coming."

"Less than that now. Ten days." I think of all the Feeders still traveling here, drawn by whispers of an impossible hope made real. "We have ten days to make sure they regret ever trying to clip our wings."

I start walking toward the mist that guards the chamber entrance, and after a moment, Zira follows. The silver light swallows our footsteps, and I let myself disappear into it, thinking of lists and contingencies and all the ways this could go right.

Because for the first time in centuries, Feeders aren't just surviving.

We're preparing for war.

Part Four: A Touch That Ignites

Chapter 25
BREE

I wake naked on floor cushions.

Velvet under my skin. Warm. Too warm.

My body hums like I've been running, like I've been touched everywhere.

For a moment I can't tell if I'm breathing or if the air is breathing me.

Something moves beyond the edge of the light.

A shape—tall, human—dark hair catching the faint glow of Ether that still drifts above the cushions.

I blink once, twice. The shape doesn't vanish.

A ghost, then.

Of course it's a ghost. Everything here is ghosts.

I let my eyes close again.

Heat rolls through me in slow, lazy waves.

Memory, maybe. His hands sliding down my back. His mouth at my throat.

The low voice that told me I was made for surrender.

Every nerve answers as if it's happening again. My hips tilt. My breath catches.

The cushions exhale silver light and my Ether follows—soft, obedient, dark at the edges.

A whisper brushes my ear: *good girl.*

I arch toward it before I remember there's no one here.

When I open my eyes, the ghost is closer.

Kneeling now. Close enough that I can almost make out a face.

My heart trips over itself. "No…" The sound is barely a breath.

It can't be him. I killed him. I saw—

The thought unravels before it can finish.

The memory drags me back under.

Shadow against skin. The press of teeth where my pulse lives.

Pleasure sharp enough to burn.

I reach for air that isn't there and moan into the dark.

My Ether rises in thin, luminous threads, answering hunger with hunger.

Every pulse makes the silver dimmer.

I should be afraid of that, but all I feel is want.

Footsteps again. Closer.

I twist onto my side, half-asleep, half-remembering. Fingers—his fingers—draw patterns between my thighs.

My body trembles, chasing sensation that might be dream, might be memory, might be both.

The cushions slide beneath me. The air tastes sweet and metallic.

I come with a sound that isn't mine, Ether flooding outward in black-rimmed light.

For a heartbeat the ghost's face flares in that light—shock, awe, pain.

Then everything fades.

When I blink, he's beside me. Real enough to cast a shadow.

Real enough that the cold from him feels like air after fire.

My hand lifts without thinking, reaching for warmth that isn't here anymore.

But the ghost's fingers brush mine instead.

Light bursts—silver threaded with black. Beautiful. Wrong.

It wraps around us like smoke, twining from my wrist to his.

He shudders, eyes going wide, mouth parting as if to speak.

No sound comes out—only a gasp that tears through the quiet like a prayer.

I feel something pull from me, something essential, and still I don't let go.

The warmth fades first.

Then the light.

Then him.

He's still holding my hand when the world starts to dim.

I can feel the tremor in his fingers, the slowing rhythm of his breath.

A thread hums between us—thin, alive, unfinished.

His voice finally finds me as everything tilts toward dark.

Soft. Distant. Devoted.

"I'll find you again," he says. "However long it takes. I'll find you."

The words chase me down as I fall back into the dream.

Back to the silk. The hands. The heat.

Back to belonging.

I don't notice the Ether dimming around me, or how his body goes still beside the cushions.

I just sink into the warmth, sighing like I've come home.

Maybe I'm sleeping.

Maybe I'm awake.

I can't tell anymore.

All I know is I want to go back.

Chapter 26
SETH

The pull jerks me forward one final time, and the Void shifts around me.

Not gone. Still here. But different.

The darkness thickens into walls—black stone, silver fire flickering without heat. The oppressive emptiness becomes a chamber, and the air tastes like smoke and something sweeter underneath.

Ethos's chamber.

Terror floods through me because I know this place. Know what happens here. Know I should turn around and run before he—

Then I see her.

Every thought scatters like ash.

She's lying on floor cushions in a pool of silver light, naked and trembling, and she's the most beautiful thing I've ever seen.

Not beautiful like art or distant stars. Beautiful like water after years of drought. Like the first breath after drowning.

Beautiful like hope I'd forgotten existed.

Her dark hair spills across velvet, and even from here I can see the way her chest rises and falls, fast and shallow. Her skin glows faintly in the dim light, and silver threads drift around her like she's exhaling magic with every breath.

But there's black threading through the silver.

A lot of black.

My stomach drops.

I know what that means. I've seen it before, in the others who crossed through and didn't make it. The ones who heard Ethos's voice and followed it into corruption.

But never like this.

Never this cruel.

Because she's not awake. Not really. Her eyes are closed, lips parted, and her body moves like she's responding to touch that isn't there. Like she's trapped in something that feels real enough to drown in.

He's feeding off her dreams.

The realization hits me like a fist to the gut.

Not just feeding—replacing reality with something that feels better than truth. Making her want the cage so much she won't try to escape it.

It's the cruelest thing I've ever seen him do.

And I've seen a lot.

A sound escapes her—soft, broken, wanting—and something in my chest cracks wide open.

I should leave. Should back away slowly and disappear into the Void before Ethos realizes I'm here.

But I can't.

My feet move without permission, carrying me closer to the cushions. Closer to her.

She doesn't notice. Doesn't even open her eyes.

Just lies there trembling, chasing sensations that aren't real, while the silver around her dims with every breath.

I kneel at the edge of the light, close enough now to see the details that make her real instead of dream.

Freckles scattered across her nose and cheeks. The way her fingers curl into the velvet like she's holding onto something.

And scars.

So many scars.

They cover her body like a map of pain—pale lines across her ribs, a cluster on her shoulder blade, more scattered down her arms and thighs. Some are old, silvered with time. Others look newer, angrier.

My heart breaks all over again.

Because it's not just this. Not just Ethos and his cruel dream-feeding.

She's survived a lifetime of torture.

Her story is written on her skin in violence, and she's still here. Still breathing. Still reaching for something even when she's lost in nightmares.

She's real.

And she's the strongest thing I've ever seen.

I let out a breath I didn't know I was holding.

The emptiness I've carried for years—decades, maybe—and the scars she wears on her skin. They're the same thing, aren't they? Different kinds of survival. Different kinds of torture that should have broken us but didn't.

She's the first real thing I've seen in longer than I can remember.

The silver Ether drifts closer to me, curious and cautious all at once. A tendril brushes my arm and I freeze, expecting pain or cold or the hollow ache the Void leaves behind.

Instead, it feels warm.

Safe.

Like recognition.

More threads follow, wrapping around my wrist, my forearm, curling up toward my chest like they're searching for something. The black is there too, woven through the silver, but it doesn't feel malicious. Just... lost. Confused.

Like her.

The Ether tightens slightly, and for the first time in years—longer than years—I don't feel alone.

I don't know what this means. Don't understand why her magic would reach for someone like me—powerless, trapped, insignificant.

But it does.

And I can't make myself pull away.

"No..."

Her voice is barely a whisper, but it makes me jerk backward anyway.

Her eyes flutter open for just a moment, unfocused and glassy, and they land somewhere near where I'm kneeling.

She's looking at me.

Or through me.

I can't tell which.

"It can't be him," she breathes. "I killed him."

The words don't make sense, but before I can try to understand them, her eyes are already closing again.

She thinks I'm someone else.

Someone she killed.

For a moment, her face twists with something that looks like grief. Like guilt.

Then it smooths.

The dream takes her again—I can see it happen. The way her expression shifts from pain to something else entirely. Her lips part. Her breathing changes, deepening.

She's not here anymore. Not seeing me or remembering whoever she thought I was.

She's back in whatever Ethos showed her. Whatever he made her feel.

I stay frozen, barely breathing, as she twists onto her side. Her body reacts to memories I can't see. Her breath catches. Her hips tilt. A soft sound escapes her throat that has nothing to do with grief and everything to do with want.

The Ether wraps tighter around me, and I let it.

Because even lost in dreams, even broken and corrupted and bleeding magic like an open wound, she's reaching for me.

Or her magic is, at least.

She comes apart right there in front of me.

Her back arches, lips parting on a moan, and her Ether floods outward in a wave of black-rimmed light that washes over me.

For one impossible moment, I feel everything.

Her pleasure. Her confusion. Her want all tangled up with shame and surrender.

And underneath it all—buried so deep she probably doesn't even know it's there—terror.

The light flares so bright I have to close my eyes.

When I open them again, she's looking at me.

Really looking this time.

Her hand lifts—trembling, uncertain—and reaches toward me.

Not toward where Ethos was. Not toward the memory.

Toward me.

I don't think. Don't hesitate.

I reach back.

Our fingers brush, and the world explodes.

Light bursts from the contact point—silver and black and something else that feels alive. Her Ether wraps around both our hands like binding, like claiming, like something permanent and terrifying and perfect all at once.

Ecstasy shoots through me so sharp it borders on pain.

I gasp, body jerking forward, and for the first time in longer than I can remember, I feel *full*.

Connected.

Alive.

But there's pain too—deep and visceral, like something vital is being pulled out through my skin. Like her magic is feeding on whatever small spark of life I have left.

I don't care.

Let it take everything.

Let her take all that I am.

As long as I get to feel this for one more second—

The light fades slowly, reluctantly.

I'm shaking. My whole body trembles like I've been struck by lightning, and I can barely breathe around the sensation still echoing through my bones.

But I'm still holding her hand.

A thread hums between us now. Thin. Alive. Unfinished.

I don't know what it means, but I can feel it like a tether pulling tight.

Her eyes start to flutter closed again.

"I'll find you again." The words tear out of me, rough and desperate and more honest than anything I've ever said. "However long it takes. I'll find you."

She doesn't respond.

Just sighs softly and sinks deeper into the cushions, her face smoothing into something that looks like peace.

Her hand goes slack in mine.

The Ether around her dims, and I watch in horror as the silver fades almost completely beneath the black.

She's still breathing. Still alive.

But barely.

And I can't do anything to stop it.

I need to leave. Need to get out of here before Ethos returns and finds me with her.

But I can't make myself let go of her hand.

The thread between us pulls tight, humming with something I don't understand.

I force myself to release her fingers, and the loss feels like tearing something vital.

The Ether clings to me for one more moment before reluctantly retreating back to her.

Like it doesn't want to let me go either.

I push to my feet, legs unsteady, and back away from the cushions.

Every instinct screams at me to stay. To protect her. To do something.

But I'm powerless here. Insignificant. If Ethos finds me, I'm dead.

Or worse.

I take one last look at her—naked and vulnerable and so beautiful it makes my chest ache—and commit every detail to memory.

The way her hair falls across the velvet. The rise and fall of her chest. The faint glow of corrupted Ether still drifting around her like a shroud.

"I'll find you," I whisper again, even though she can't hear me anymore.

Then I turn and run.

The chamber melts back into Void as I flee, darkness swallowing the stone walls and silver fire. But the thread stays intact, pulling tight across the distance.

She's still there. Still connected.

Still mine, somehow.

I don't stop running until the chamber is far behind me and the oppressive emptiness of the Void closes in again.

Only then do I let myself collapse, gasping, shaking, every nerve still singing with the aftershock of her touch.

The thread hums faintly in my chest.

A compass.

A promise.

A way to find her again.

However long it takes.

Chapter 27
BREE

I wake hollow.

Everything feels scooped out. Empty veins. Bones that ache like they remember being pulled apart.

I know the cushions are soft beneath me, but I barely feel them. The Ether drifts around me, tired and thin. When I reach for it, nothing happens. Just that muffled hum under my skin that won't answer.

But there's something else.

A warmth. Low in my chest. Small. Steady. Not mine.

Gray's voice whispers through my mind, quiet and certain: *"Love."*

The memory flickers and fades before I can hold onto it.

I press my palm to my chest, trying to catch it. Trying to remember. But it's gone, slipping away like smoke.

Maybe it's what he left behind. When he—

Ethos.

Heat crawls through me before I can finish the thought. His hands. His mouth. The way he made me feel like I mattered.

I want that again.

It should feel wrong. It doesn't. Just feels hungry.

The warmth pulses and I sink into it, letting it wrap around me like I deserve it.

My legs shake when I stand, but they hold.

The chamber is quieter now. Silver fire dimmed to almost nothing. Black stone that should feel oppressive but doesn't anymore. Or maybe I'm just used to it.

My eyes find the mirror.

I don't mean to look. Don't decide to move toward it. But I do anyway.

One step. Then another. Like something's pulling me.

Not curiosity. Not fear. Need.

My feet carry me across cold stone, and the Ether follows slow and tired, black threads weaving through silver. It should worry me. It doesn't.

Rhett's laugh echoes somewhere distant, warm like fire.

I reach for it, but it slips away like smoke.

I stop in front of the glass and stare at my reflection.

She looks different. More certain. Eyes still green but flickering like static.

The warmth flares in my chest.

I gasp, my hand flying up. My reflection does the same, but slower. Like she's moving through water while I move through air.

"Why can't I stop?" I whisper to the empty chamber.

The mirror doesn't answer.

The warmth pulses again, stronger this time. It pulls—not toward something, but toward the glass itself. Like gravity. Like recognition.

I lift my hand without thinking and press my palm flat to the surface.

It hums.

Faint, but real. I feel it vibrate against my skin, feel the way the glass shifts slightly under my touch. Not quite solid, not quite liquid. Something between.

The warmth in my chest flares bright enough to hurt.

For just a second I see something in the reflection behind me. A shadow. A shape.

A face I recognize but shouldn't. Dark hair. Eyes that looked at me like I mattered.

Seth.

But I killed him. Didn't I?

The thought fractures before it finishes.

Gone.

I pull back, breathing hard. What was that?

The hunger twists tighter, and I don't know what I'm craving anymore. His touch? His voice? Or something else entirely?

Jace's voice cuts through sharp with worry: *"We've got you."*

The words dissolve before they finish forming.

The warmth pulses like an answer I can't read.

I press my palm to the mirror again, desperate to understand. I need to know why I can't look away, why the glass feels alive under my hand, why every time the warmth flares I feel less alone.

Maybe it's him. Maybe he's so deep inside me now that even mirrors call with his voice.

It should terrify me. Instead, it makes me lean closer.

The temperature drops.

I spin around, jerking my hand back. The warmth flickers like a candle in wind.

He's here.

I feel him before I see him. The air thickening. Light shifting black-blue. My body reacting before my mind catches up—fear and want colliding so hard I can't breathe.

"Still staring at yourself, little Queen?"

His voice comes first, smooth and cold and perfect. Then he's there, materializing from shadow, and I have to force myself not to step toward him.

He's beautiful. That's the worst part.

The warmth in my chest pulses sharp and sudden.

I gasp.

His eyes flicker with something that looks like satisfaction.

"There it is," he murmurs, moving closer. Circling me like a predator studying prey. "That spark. That hunger."

I can't answer. Can't think past the way my body responds. Heat pooling low even as some distant part of me screams to run.

Thane's voice cuts through, cold and sharp: *Little queen.*

But it sounds wrong. Too warm. Like a memory trying to become real.

It slips away.

His fingers brush my jaw, tilting my face up to meet his gaze.

"You're exquisite," he says, and it sounds like worship and possession all at once.

His thumb traces my lower lip, and the warmth flares again.

The sound that escapes me—half gasp, half moan—I don't recognize it.

His smile sharpens.

"See?" His voice drops lower, intimate. "Even your magic knows who you belong to."

The words settle into my bones like truth.

Because he's right. Isn't he?

The hunger. The pull. The way I can't stop wanting him even when I know I should.

That's all him. All his influence threading through me until I can't tell where I end and he begins.

Even this warmth—this foreign pulse in my chest—must be another thread he's woven. Another way he's claimed me.

His hand slides from my jaw to my throat, not squeezing, just resting there. Possessive.

"The Council is preparing to meet," he says, his voice steady and rhythmic. Each word designed to drown thought. "They believe you're lost. That the sanctuary failed."

My breath catches. The sanctuary. The guys.

Wes's quiet voice whispers through my mind: *"Beautiful."*

It hurts to hear. Hurts worse when it fades.

"They've moved on, little queen." His thumb strokes once across my pulse. "Convinced themselves you made your choice."

The words twist like knives.

"But I stayed." His eyes lock on mine. "I'm the only one who knows what you really need. The only one who can make you feel what you deserve."

Each sentence pulls me back under, unraveling whatever fragile thread of independence I almost regained.

Maybe he's right. Maybe they did give up.

Stellan's voice drifts through, elegant and precise: *"Darling."*

The word aches. I reach for it desperately, but it dissolves like mist.

Theo's voice follows, certain and gentle: *"We see you, Bree."*

But they don't. Not anymore.

Maybe I'm only worth something when I'm broken enough to need him.

The warmth pulses weakly, like protest. I barely feel it beneath the weight of his words.

His hand moves from my throat to my hair, fingers tangling gently. Possessively.

"Look at yourself," he murmurs, turning me back toward the mirror.

I do.

My reflection stares back. The Ether around her is more black than silver now, moving with purpose and control I've never had before.

She looks powerful. Dangerous.

I remember standing here before. Staring at myself in the black silk. Thinking I looked like Riley—confident, certain, everything I wasn't.

I thought I was pretending. Playing dress-up.

But I see it now. I wasn't trying to be her.

She was showing me what I could become.

What I was always meant to be.

His.

For just a moment, I swear I see another hand beside mine in the glass. Different. Unfamiliar.

Then it's gone.

Ethos doesn't notice. He's already speaking again, his voice a constant pressure that leaves no room for other thoughts.

"Tomorrow, I want you again." His breath is warm against my ear. "I need you."

I should say no. Should pull away.

Instead, I just nod. Or maybe I don't. Maybe my silence is just heavy enough that it feels like consent.

His smile curves against my temple. "Good girl."

The warmth flickers once more, weaker now. Barely there.

I let it fade beneath the hunger that feels like coming home. Beneath the certainty that this is where I belong.

I don't notice when he steps back into shadow. Don't register when the chamber grows darker.

I just stand there staring at my reflection. At the black Ether curling around me like smoke. At the girl who finally knows what she wants. At the girl who is finally everything she always wanted to be.

Even if what she wants will destroy her.

Chapter 28
SETH

I'm still shaking.

Not from cold—the Void doesn't have temperature. Except for that god forsaken chamber *she* was in. But from whatever just happened, whatever that was, when something locked into place so final that my entire body felt like it was being torn apart and rewritten at the same time.

The thread in my chest hums. Steady. Real.

I press my palm flat against my sternum, half expecting to feel something physical—a mark, a scar, anything that proves what just happened wasn't my mind finally breaking.

Nothing. Just skin and bone and that impossible hum beneath both.

"What the hell is it?" I whisper to the darkness.

No answer. Just the pulse, rhythmic and insistent, like a second heartbeat I didn't ask for but can't live without now.

The Void feels different.

Not empty anymore. Not pressing in on me like it's trying to decide whether to consume or ignore me.

It's... listening.

That thought should terrify me. Instead, I just feel exhausted.

I slump against something that might be a wall or might be nothing at all. My legs give out and I slide down, arms wrapping around my knees.

"Just need a minute," I mutter. "Just one goddamn minute."

The hum synchronizes with my breathing. In, out. Steady. Like it's trying to calm me down or maybe remind me I'm not alone anymore.

I close my eyes.

Sleep shouldn't be possible here. But my body doesn't care what should or shouldn't be possible. It just shuts down, dragging me under before I can fight it.

After what could be minutes or hours, a sound pulls me back.

Soft. Rhythmic. Pads on stone.

My eyes snap open, heart hammering, every muscle tensed to run.

Ethos. Or worse—one of those things that screams without sound, the ones that hunt anything stupid enough to move.

But the shape that steps from the shadows is small.

Made of shadow that moves like smoke but holds its form. A fox. Eyes that burn like tiny stars in a face made of living darkness.

It sits a few feet away and tilts its head at me.

Curious. Not predatory.

"You're not real," I whisper.

The fox yawns, showing sharp white teeth, then settles back on its haunches like it's got all the time in the world.

My breath comes fast. Shallow. Every instinct screaming at me to move, to run, to do anything except stand here waiting to be devoured.

But it doesn't move. Just watches me with those burning eyes.

When I shift a little, testing, it doesn't flee or attack.

It walks right up to me.

I freeze.

Its nose nudges my hand—warm, solid, real—and I jerk back like I've been burned.

Void creatures don't touch without devouring. They don't have warmth. They don't—

The fox just sits again, tail flicking through the air, leaving faint trails of silver light that fade as soon as they appear.

The darkness around it stays still. Doesn't writhe or pulse or consume.

It's just... there.

"You shouldn't exist," I mutter.

The fox's ears twitch, like it's amused.

The thread in my chest hums louder, matching the rhythm of the light trailing from the fox's tail.

Oh.

Oh god.

A flutter interrupts the silence.

I look up and a raven descends from nowhere—because there's no sky here, no ceiling, just endless black.

Wings made of shadow and night, feathers that seem to drink light rather than reflect it. It lands on the fox's back, then hops down to the ground, studying me with the same curious intensity.

It cocks its head and lets out a single sharp cry.

The hum in my chest answers.

I clutch at my sternum, gasping. "What are you?"

The fox and bird exchange a glance—too deliberate, too coordinated to be random.

Then they both turn to look at something in the distance.

I follow their gaze.

There—faint, barely visible—mirror-like surfaces glinting in the darkness. Lined up like doorways. Like a path.

The Void has never had direction before.

"No," I whisper. "No, this isn't—"

Movement at my wrist.

Cold. Smooth. Deliberate.

I look down just as a small serpent materializes from shadow, sleek and impossible. It coils around my wrist—not tight, but firm.

Like a bracelet. Like a claim.

I freeze, expecting the bite. Expecting pain.

Instead, it settles and hums.

The same rhythm as the thread in my chest.

Warmth floods through the contact—not heat, but energy. Recognition. The same surge I felt when she reached for me, when something snapped into place.

The snake lifts its head, tongue flicking, eyes silver-bright.

All three creatures hum together. The air vibrates softly around us, synchronized and purposeful.

"You're hers," I breathe. "You're hers, aren't you?"

The fox's tail swishes once.

The raven lets out another sharp cry.

The snake tightens slightly, just enough to confirm.

They're Void creatures. Born from this darkness.

But they're hers too.

Shadow and silver merged into something new.

And now they're here for me.

Protecting me. Guiding me.

The fox stands, shakes itself once, and begins walking toward the distant mirrors.

The bird takes flight, circling above in lazy loops that leave silver trails across the darkness.

The snake's hum pulses against my wrist like a heartbeat.

The darkness parts under their feet. Silver ripples radiate outward with each step, like they're walking on water that reflects light that shouldn't exist.

"Where are you taking me?" I whisper.

The fox looks back once, expression almost impatient.

Come on. We don't have time for this.

I get to my feet. Legs unsteady but obeying.

Each step I take, the Void responds. Bends slightly. Shifts.

It's alive.

It's listening.

And for the first time since I was lost, the Void isn't empty.

It's waiting.

The fox leads.

The bird calls.

The snake hums against my pulse.

And I follow.

Chapter 29
SETH

The fox leads and I follow.

Because why the hell not?

The raven circles overhead, calling out every so often. Each cry leaves a shimmer of silver static that ripples through the darkness like sound made visible.

The snake around my wrist shifts occasionally, scales glowing faintly in sync with the hum in my chest.

The Void isn't silent anymore. Every step sounds like walking on the surface of a vast lake—hollow and resonant and alive.

"You really think she's this way?" I whisper.

The fox glances back as if to say, *You already know she is.*

The path ahead glows faintly with reflected silver light, forming ripples that stretch into infinity. The deeper we go, the louder the hum becomes—steady, guiding, insistent.

I don't know how long we walk. Time doesn't work here.

But eventually, the darkness shifts.

Mirrors appear in the distance. Hundreds of them. Thousands, maybe.

What is going on?

Freestanding, cracked, floating slightly above the black surface like they're suspended in water. All sizes, all shapes, all reflecting nothing but more darkness.

The fox leads me to one in particular.

Tall, but not floor-to-ceiling. Black iron frame with scrollwork that twists into sharp points like horns.

I stop dead.

There's something wrong about it. The frame looks hungry—like it's drinking the darkness around it instead of reflecting it.

"No."

The word comes out rough, barely audible.

The fox sits and stares. The snake hums harder against my wrist. The raven circles above, crying out.

The mirror surface ripples faintly, and I can see through it.

Not Ethos's chamber. Not where she's trapped.

A different chamber. Larger. Ancient. Filled with mirrors lining curved walls.

Empty. Waiting.

My throat closes.

Still I find myself reaching out instinctively, fingers brushing the cold metal frame.

The mirror responds. Silver ripples spread outward from where my hand touches the surface, and the hum in my chest flares so bright it hurts.

It's not showing me where she is.

It's showing me a way out.

"No," I say again, backing away. "I'm not leaving her. You hear me? I won't."

The fox growls softly, pushing against my leg.

The raven lands on my shoulder, pecking once—not to hurt, but to insist.

The snake tightens around my wrist, the hum vibrating painfully now.

"She's still there," I grit out. "If I leave—if I go through—what if I can't get back to her?"

The fox's eyes flare bright silver. The air trembles.

The mirror flashes once, too bright, then pulses like a heartbeat.

The snake lets out a sharp hiss. The hum in my chest spikes, and the mirror surface bursts outward like water splashing in reverse.

I stumble forward, trying to stop myself, but the creatures surge with me—the fox and raven dissolve into light, the snake coils tighter, dragging me through.

I scream as everything turns inside out—

—and then I'm falling.

I slam into the ground hard, gasping, choking on air that tastes real.

Dust. Stone. Magic.

Everything's too loud. Too bright.

I touch the floor beneath me, whispering, "This... isn't the Void."

The words sound strange out loud. Foreign.

The hum in my chest is quieter now but still there. The snake is still wrapped around my wrist, faintly glowing.

I push myself up slowly, legs shaking. The chamber breathes around me—alive with magic I can feel resonating through the walls, humming at the same frequency as the connection in my chest.

The mirror I just came through shimmers once, then goes still.

Footsteps echo.

Urgent.

I turn, and a figure appears at the edge of the chamber.

Tall. Pale. Elegant in a way that feels dangerous.

He stops dead when he sees me. Goes completely still.

Then his face drains of color.

"No." The word comes out like he's been punched. "No, you're—"

"Who are you?" I ask, voice rough from disuse.

He doesn't answer. Just stares at me like I'm something impossible.

"Seth." He breathes the name in recognition.

Another pause.

"How do you know my name?" I press.

That breaks through his shock. His eyes sharpen, dangerous now.

"Because I watched you die." His voice is cold, controlled. "I watched Bree's Ether tear through you. Watched you burn away to nothing when Phil—" He cuts himself off.

"I don't know who Phil is." My stomach drops. "I don't know what you're talking about. I've been trapped in the Void. I don't know how long. Years. Maybe decades." I press my hand to my chest, trying to ground myself. "Time doesn't work there."

Something shifts in his expression. Understanding, maybe. Or horror.

"You came from the Void," he says carefully. "Were you alone?"

"No. There was—" My chest tightens around the memory. "A woman. Dark hair, green eyes. Scars everywhere."

His whole body goes rigid.

"Is that her name?" I ask before he can speak, chest tightening. "Bree?" I press my hand over my heart, where the hum still pulses. "The woman..." My voice drops to something almost reverent. "She's beautiful. Even fading, even scared. The scars just make her more…" I trail off, not sure how to finish. "More."

"Yes." His voice cracks on the word, and something shifts in his expression—the dangerous edge softening. "It's Bree." He pauses, and when he speaks again there's something raw in his voice. Afraid. "She's alive? Gods, tell me she's still alive."

"Yes," I say quickly. "But she's fading. There's someone with her. Ethos. He's—feeding on her, I think. This chamber, black stone, silver fire."

Something shutters across his face—not relief. Horror.

"How bad?" His voice goes flat, cold. Dangerous.

"Bad." My throat tightens. "She's scared. Trapped. And whatever he's doing to her—" I press my hand to my chest, feeling the hum there. "I could feel it. Like she was being drained."

"Describe the scars," he says suddenly, voice urgent.

I blink, thrown by the shift. "Everywhere. Arms, shoulders, legs. Some old, some newer. She's—" My voice catches. "Beautiful. Fragile. Fading."

He closes his eyes briefly, and I realize he's confirming something.

"There's someone upstairs," he says carefully. "Claims to be Bree. Black Ether threaded with silver. No scars. And wrong."

The world tilts.

"We've known something was off," he continues, voice low. "But we couldn't prove it. If you were in the Void with the real one—"

He stops, staring at my wrist. "That creature. I saw it before. The day you… the man we thought was Seth, died. When her power exploded, shadow creatures came through. That's one of hers."

"I don't understand." My voice sounds hollow. "She's trapped in the Void, and there's someone here pretending to be her—"

"Then we have proof." His eyes are sharp now, calculating. "Someone switched places with Bree somehow."

The snake hums against my wrist.

A voice echoes faintly in my head: *Welcome home.*

"Yes." He studies the snake on my wrist. "And you're connected to her somehow."

"Something happened between us, when our fingers touched." I admit. "It felt like it locked into place. I don't know what it was, but—"

"A bond." His voice is quiet. "You bonded with her in the Void."

The word settles in my chest like an anchor.

Bree.

Hope flares in his expression, sharp and sudden. "If you came through a mirror from the Void, then there's a way. We just need to figure out how to get her back."

I look at the mirror behind me, still and dark now.

"The creatures led me here," I say. "They knew the way."

"Then they can lead us back." He's already moving, pacing, thinking.

"What if they won't?"

His smile is cold. Sharp.

"Then we make them want to."

The snake hums against my wrist, and I feel that pull again—faint but there. The connection threading back through the mirror, back to the Void, back to her.

Back to Bree.

"We're going to get her out," he says, and it sounds like a promise. Like an oath.

I nod, something fierce and desperate rising in my chest.

"Yeah," I whisper. "We are."

Part Five: Trust The Process

Chapter 30
THANE

My phone vibrates in my pocket.

Stellan's name flashes across the screen.

I almost ignore it—I'm in the middle of watching the imposter through the window, cataloging every tell, every wrong movement that proves she isn't who she pretends to be. But something about the timing makes me answer.

"What."

"You need to get to the chamber." His voice is clipped. Sharp. Wrong. "Now."

I go still. Stellan doesn't sound like that unless something's gone catastrophically wrong.

"What happened?"

"You'll want to see this for yourself." A pause, weighted. "And bring Zira."

The line goes dead.

I stare at the phone for three seconds, then move.

Zira's already waiting by the stairs when I find her, arms crossed, expression unreadable.

"He called you too," I say.

"Five minutes ago." Her gray eyes are sharp. Focused. "Told me to wait for you."

That alone is enough to make my stomach drop. The three of us have been working together for a week—coordinating the Feeders coming through, managing the Oath complications, keeping the imposter distracted. Stellan doesn't pull us both in like this unless something's shifted.

We descend in silence.

The stairwell grows colder with every step, air turning metallic. The old wards hum against my skin—active, alert, responding to something they recognize.

"You feel that?" Zira mutters.

I nod. "Something's changed."

Wrong. Too strong. Too alive.

At the final turn, I catch Stellan's voice echoing off stone—low, soothing, the tone he uses with frightened fledglings who don't understand what they've become yet.

My instincts sharpen. Every nerve in my body goes taut.

I round the corner into the chamber, and everything stops.

The scent hits me first.

Old blood. Ether residue. And something else—cold that shouldn't exist in physical form. The kind of empty that tastes like the Void.

Then I see him.

Standing near the black iron mirror, wild-eyed and lean. Pale skin that looks like it hasn't seen real light in years. Dark hair falling into his face. The snake—Bree's familiar—coiled around his wrist, glowing faintly silver.

And when he turns toward me—

"You."

The word rips out of me like a snarl.

Seth flinches, and his lips pull back instinctively.

Fangs.

Sharp. White. Unmistakable.

My world narrows to a single point of rage.

I'm across the chamber before conscious thought catches up, hand closing around his throat, slamming him back against the mirror hard enough to rattle the glass.

The surface ripples behind him, silver light spilling across us both.

"Thane!" Stellan's voice cuts through the static in my head. "Stop!"

But I can't.

Because this is him. This is the man who betrayed her, who worked with Phil, who stood there and let her power tear through him while he smiled—

Except.

Seth's eyes flash—not human, not quite vampire. Something in between.

The snake on his wrist glows brighter, wrapping tighter around his arm like a living shield.

My hand grows cold where it touches his throat. Not temperature—something deeper. Like the Void itself is pushing back through his skin.

My grip loosens—not because I want it to, but because the wrongness makes my instincts scream.

"What—" Seth's voice comes out rough, panicked. His free hand flies to his mouth, touching his own teeth like he's never felt them before. "What the hell—why do I have—"

He stares at me, horror bleeding across his face.

"What's happening to me?" His voice cracks. "What the fuck am I?"

I freeze.

Because that's not the reaction of someone who knows. That's terror. Confusion. The kind of fear that only comes from waking up in a body that doesn't make sense anymore.

"Thane." Stellan's hand closes on my shoulder, firm. "Let him go."

I don't move.

"Now."

Something in his tone cuts through. I release Seth's throat, stepping back but not far. Every muscle still coiled, ready to strike if he so much as breathes wrong.

Seth sags against the mirror, one hand pressed to his chest, the other still touching his fangs like he can't believe they're real.

"He's not just a vampire," Zira says from behind me, voice steady and clinical.

I snap my head toward her. "I can see that."

Stellan moves closer to Seth, studying him with that careful intensity he reserves for things he doesn't fully understand yet. He reaches out, stops just short of touching Seth's arm.

"Feel the air around him," Stellan says quietly.

I force myself to focus past the rage.

The cold isn't coming from the chamber.

It's coming from Seth.

Not physical cold. The absence kind. The kind that tastes like nothing and everything at once. The kind that lives in the spaces between worlds.

"Void," I say flatly.

Stellan nods. "He reeks of it."

"What the hell is he?" I demand.

Zira steps forward, tilting her head as she studies Seth like a scholar facing a living myth.

"He's bonded." Her voice carries certainty. "The snake proves it—Bree's familiar wouldn't stay with him otherwise. But something else happened too." She pauses. "I've heard about this. When a bond forms outside the human realm... sometimes the magic doesn't follow rules. It adapts to the environment. Alters the Feeder's base nature."

"You're saying the Void changed him."

"No." Zira meets my eyes. "The bond did. The Void just gave it room to grow."

Seth shakes his head, backing away from all three of us until his shoulders hit the mirror again.

"I don't know what you're talking about." His voice is raw. Desperate. "I just—she was dying, I think—and then—" He touches his chest, right over his heart. "It hurt. It felt like everything inside me broke and rebuilt itself."

The word *she* cuts through everything else.

"Bree." My voice comes out flat. Controlled.

Seth's gaze jerks to me. "You're—" He pauses, uncertain. Afraid. "You know her too?"

"Thane." I force the word out. "And yes. She's mine."

Stellan clears his throat. "Stellan. And she's *ours*, actually."

I shoot him a look but don't contradict it. Because right now, that's the only truth that matters.

The rage drains out of me all at once, leaving only awe and grief.

"She's alive." My voice sounds strange to my own ears. Hollow. Hopeful. "You found her. And you bonded her in the Void."

Silence.

The mirror behind Seth ripples faintly, responding to his presence.

All four of us feel it.

Stellan glances toward the glass, something calculating in his expression. "That's our path back, isn't it?"

Seth's face goes pale. "I—I don't know. The creatures led me here once, but I didn't control it. They just—" He gestures helplessly at the mirror. "I don't know if I can do it again. If I can open it."

"You will," I say, and it comes out harder than I mean it to. "You came through once. You'll do it again."

"And if I can't?" His voice cracks. "What if I try and it doesn't work? What if—"

"Then we figure it out." Stellan's voice is calm. Certain. "But you're going to try."

I step forward, forcing myself to meet his eyes without violence.

"You're going to take us to her."

Seth nods, shaky but resolute. "I'll try."

The chamber settles into uneasy quiet, the mirror behind Seth still rippling like disturbed water.

Zira speaks into the silence. "Whatever magic created you, it did so for a reason. The Void doesn't give gifts. It trades."

I hold Seth's gaze for a long moment. Conflict and fury and reluctant respect warring within me.

Because he came back. He found a way through the Void and came back for her.

That has to mean something.

"We need to talk to the others," Stellan says, breaking the silence. "All of them."

I tense. "Not yet. We don't know—"

"They deserve to know," Stellan cuts me off, voice firm. "Seth's alive. Bree's alive. And we have a way to reach her." His gray eyes are steady, unyielding. "You can't keep this from them."

I want to argue. Want to control the narrative, manage the fallout, keep everything contained until I understand what we're dealing with.

But he's right.

"Fine." The word tastes bitter. "But we do this carefully."

Stellan glances at Seth, then back at me. "He's coming too."

"What?" The word comes out sharp.

"He's hers, Thane." Stellan's voice is calm but firm. "Bonded. Just like you. They need to meet him. See he's not a threat."

My jaw clenches, but I can't argue with the logic. Seth is bonded to Bree. That makes him part of this whether I like it or not.

"This is going to be a disaster," I mutter.

Zira lets out a low whistle from across the chamber. "Better you than me." She's already backing toward the far wall, clearly planning to stay well clear of whatever's about to happen.

Stellan moves toward the stairs. "I'll get them."

Seth looks between us, still shaky, still confused. "What are you going to tell them?"

"The truth," I say flatly. "That you're alive. That you found her. And that we're going to get her back."

His throat works. "They're going to hate me."

"Probably." I don't soften it. Wouldn't be fair to him. "But you're going to have to face them anyway."

I watch Stellan disappear up the stairs, then turn back to Seth.

He's still pressed against the mirror, looking like he might bolt if given half a chance. The snake around his wrist glows softly, a living tether to someone who isn't here.

"They'll never believe it," I say quietly, more to myself than to him. "And I don't know if I do, either."

But the cold radiating off Seth says otherwise. The Void-touched emptiness that clings to him like a second skin.

The bond is real. The Void changed him. And somewhere, on the other side of that mirror, Bree is waiting.

We just have to figure out how to reach her before it's too late.

Chapter 31
JACE

I'm half-asleep on the couch when Stellan appears in the doorway like a ghost with a death wish.

"Where's Bree?" he asks, voice low and sharp.

"Went to bed early," Rhett says from the kitchen doorway, drying his hands on a towel. "Said something about needing her beauty sleep."

Stellan's jaw tightens. "Good. Keep it that way." His eyes sweep over the room. "All of you need to come with me. Now. And don't let her hear you."

I blink, pushing myself up from the couch. "What's going on?"

"Just move, Jace."

That's when I notice the others filtering in from various corners of the sanctuary—Gray from the library, Wes from upstairs. Theo's already in the hallway, looking like he hasn't slept in days.

Nobody's joking. Nobody's asking questions.

That alone makes my stomach drop.

"Since when do we whisper in our own house?" I mutter, falling into step behind Stellan.

"Since the dead came back," he says without looking back.

My stomach drops into my shoes. My heart stays where it was—halfway to breaking.

We follow him out of the sanctuary and into the tree line, tension thick enough to choke on. Rhett burns quiet beside me, steam rising from his skin in the cold air. Wes goes pale behind us. The rest of us follow the sound of Stellan's shoes.

"What do you think this is about?" I murmur to Rhett.

"No idea," he mutters back. "But if something's wrong with Bree—"

"Not now," Stellan snaps without turning around. His voice is sharp enough to cut. "Save it for the chamber."

Rhett's jaw tightens, heat flickering beneath his skin. "If you dragged us out of here for nothing—"

"I said save it." Stellan stops at the top of the stairs leading down to the chamber, turning to face us. His gray eyes are cold, harder than I've ever seen them. "What's down there changes everything. So I need you all to shut up and listen before you react."

"You can't just—" Wes starts.

"I can," Stellan cuts him off. "And I am. Because if you go down there already defensive about her, you won't hear what needs to be said."

The way he says *her* makes my stomach drop.

"What the hell is that supposed to mean?" Rhett demands.

Stellan doesn't back down. "It means you're about to have your world shattered, and I need you functional when it happens. Not burning the sanctuary down because you can't handle the truth."

Silence. Heavy and suffocating.

Then Stellan turns and heads down the stairs.

Every step echoes like we're walking into our own grave.

Theo keeps pressing his fingers to his temple. I want to crack a joke. Something about midnight incubus summons or secret cult meetings. But the words die in my throat because Stellan's walking like he's heading into a war zone, and Thane's already waiting at the bottom of the stairs.

And so is someone else.

The figure stands in the center of the chamber, gaunt, hollow-eyed, clothes torn by hell itself.

Dark hair. Pale skin. A snake coiled around his wrist—glowing the way her magic used to.

When I see his eyes, my breath stops.

"You're dead," Rhett says, voice flat.

Seth lifts his head slowly, like even that small movement costs him. "That wasn't me."

The room fractures—Rhett stepping forward, Gray catching his arm, Wes making a sound halfway between gasp and sob. My own heart pounds so hard it hurts.

"What the hell does that mean?" I manage.

Thane steps forward, voice measured and cold. "The Seth who died at the sanctuary was his mirror self." His silver eyes never leave Seth's face. "This is the real Seth. He's been trapped in the Void."

Stellan adds quietly, "I saw him come through the mirror myself."

Seth's gaze drifts over us, tired and haunted. His eyes linger on Thane, then Stellan—recognition there. When he looks at the rest of us, there's only confusion.

"I don't know any of you."

The words land like stones.

"That's not possible," Rhett says, voice cracking. "You lived at the sanctuary. You—"

"That wasn't me," Seth says quietly. "I've been trapped since I was eighteen." He swallows hard. "I don't even know how long that's been. Time doesn't work there."

Silence. Heavy and suffocating.

Then Seth's expression shifts—something urgent breaking through the exhaustion.

"But I found someone there. In the Void, just before I fell through the mirror." His voice drops. "A woman. Dark hair, pale green eyes." He pauses, and when he speaks again, his words are deliberate. "And scars. So many scars."

The air leaves my lungs.

That's when Thane cuts through the silence with words that shatter everything.

"And that's why we need to talk about who's sleeping in Bree's bed."

Rage hits me like a fist to the chest.

"Fuck you," I snap.

"Watch your mouth," Rhett growls.

"You saw her too." My hands curl into fists. "That morning. In the chamber, we found her standing right there. Alive. Safe. Finally not afraid of her own shadow."

Thane doesn't flinch. His silver eyes stay steady, cold, infuriatingly calm. "We found *someone* in that chamber. The question is who."

"What the hell are you implying?" Rhett's fire sparks along his forearms.

Stellan steps forward, voice sharp. "Her Ether inverted. Her scars vanished. She speaks like someone who never went through what Bree did."

"She's stronger," I counter. "She's finally—"

"Different," Theo murmurs, and the word lands like a stone in still water.

I whirl on him. "You too?"

Theo doesn't look at me. "The way she moves now. It's not the same."

Wes's voice is barely a whisper. "She's... still her. I think."

Gray's response is quiet, deliberate. "You *think*. Not you *know*."

"She's finally herself," Rhett says, and the desperation gives him away.

"Free?" Thane's laugh is bitter. "Or replaced?"

The room erupts—voices overlapping, everyone talking about her like she's gone while I'm still bleeding from believing she's here.

"She doesn't hesitate anymore," Wes says suddenly, and everyone stops.

His voice is so quiet we all have to strain to hear him. "When I touch her. When any of us touch her. She used to pause, just for a second, like she was reminding herself it was safe." He swallows. "She doesn't do that anymore. It's like she never had to learn that touch can hurt."

"That's good," I say, and even as I say it, I hear how wrong it sounds.

"Does it?" Gray asks. "Or does it mean whoever is wearing her face never had to learn that it could hurt."

"Stop," Rhett says, fire crawling along his knuckles. "You're talking about her like she's—"

"Different," Theo answers. "Because she is. The way she walks now—shoulders back, chin lifted. Bree used to make herself smaller."

"She's planning the Council visit like a coronation," Stellan says. "Does that sound like Bree to you?"

"She tried to force me to feed," Thane says. The admission stills the room. "She pulled me close and offered her neck without hesitation. When I refused, she called me a coward."

Theo closes his eyes. "Bree would never push like that. She would be terrified of forcing anyone."

"I've been watching," Gray says, keeping it calm. "She doesn't check exits anymore. She doesn't sit with a view of the door. She doesn't scan for threats." He looks at me. "Her scars are gone, Jace. All of them."

"Whatever happened in that chamber healed her," I say.

"Healed?" Thane's voice is sharp. "Those scars were part of her. She wouldn't have wanted them gone."

"How do you know what she wanted?" Rhett's voice breaks.

"Because she told me," Wes says. "After Phil. She said the scars mattered because they meant she survived. She said removing them would be pretending it never happened. She said she'd earned them."

"Maybe she changed her mind," I try, and I hear that I don't believe it either.

"In one night?" Stellan asks. "She went into that chamber afraid and came out complete? Without a doubt in her body?"

"She's been sleeping with us," Rhett says, and his eyes move to me and then to Wes.

Wes shakes his head.

"With me and Jace, then," Rhett says. "She was confident. She moved like she'd never been afraid of intimacy."

"She was afraid," Wes says. "Always. And she chose us anyway. That was the point."

Theo looks at us, one by one. "What did she say to you after? When it was just the two of you?"

Rhett works his jaw. "She said it was perfect."

Gray repeats it quietly, as if testing the word for truth. "Perfect."

"She called being with me perfect," I say. My throat tightens. "She looked at me like I was everything she'd ever wanted and like she finally had permission to take it."

"Permission," Stellan says. "Not choice."

The distinction lands.

"Has anyone else noticed the way she talks?" Theo asks. "No hesitation. No mid-sentence self-correction. No apology." His eyes unfocus slightly. "Bree second-guessed every word."

"When I told her she was beautiful, she didn't look away," Wes says. "She asked for more. Bree used to blush."

"This one receives praise like she expected it," Gray says.

"Stop," Rhett says, almost pleading.

No one does.

"Her Ether is inverted," Thane says at last, and every head turns. "Black threaded with silver, not silver threaded with black. That isn't evolution. It's reversal."

"What does that mean?" I ask.

"It means the Ether we're seeing doesn't belong to Bree," Thane says. "It belongs to her mirror."

Rhett's hands fall. The heat leaves the room.

I think of last night—the way she held my gaze, the calm that followed, the word she used for it.

"She called it perfect," I say, and the word tastes wrong.

No one speaks.

"Fuck."

The word cuts through the silence like a knife.

Everyone turns to look at Thane. His silver eyes are wide—not with discovery, but with recognition finally landing.

"I'm an idiot." His hands curl into fists. "I know exactly who's in Bree's bed."

Silence. Waiting.

"Riley."

The name lands like a bomb.

"Who the fuck is Riley?" Rhett demands.

Thane's voice is flat. Cold. "Bree told us. That night in her bedroom after she crossed through the mirror. She woke up on the floor and said the name. Riley." He looks at each of them. "You all heard it."

"I don't..." Wes trails off, confusion and horror mixing on his face.

"None of you remember," Stellan says quietly, realization dawning. "The black Ether. She's been suppressing it from the start."

Thane looks at Stellan. "Even you."

Stellan's jaw tightens, and for once, he has nothing to say.

"And I didn't remember until right fucking now," Thane says.

Seth raises his head. "So what are we going to do about it?"

Rhett finds his voice. "We go get her. We go into the Void and bring her home."

"And the one upstairs?" I ask.

No one answers.

Chapter 32
GRAY

The question hangs in the air—*And the one upstairs?*—and nobody has an answer.

Rhett's fire has guttered out completely. His hands hang at his sides, empty of the rage that was holding him together moments ago. Jace stares at the floor like it might open up and swallow him. Wes looks like he's about to be sick.

I'm the one who has to stay rational. Someone always has to.

"Introductions first," I say, cutting through the heavy silence. My voice sounds steadier than I feel. "One problem at a time."

Seth's eyes move over each of us as I gesture to the others in turn.

"Gray. Rhett—fire elemental. Jace—air. Wes—incubus. Theo—seer."

He nods slowly, exhaustion making every movement look like it costs him. When he gets to Wes, he lingers for a moment before moving on.

"You knew my mirror," Seth says quietly.

But Rhett can't let it rest. "He was working for Phil the entire time. Bree's stalker. Council lap dog. Your mirror was feeding him information—about all of us. Everything we said, everything we did."

"He betrayed all of us," Jace adds, voice hard. "Pretended to be our friend while reporting back to that bastard."

Seth staggers back like he's been hit. "No. That's not—I wouldn't—"

"You didn't," I say. "But he did. And when Bree lost control, when her Ether exploded—your mirror was caught in it. He died."

"She killed him," Wes whispers. "Accidentally. But she's been carrying that guilt ever since."

Seth's hands shake. He presses them against his thighs, trying to steady himself. "Does she know?" His voice cracks. "That it wasn't really me?"

"Not yet," Thane says coldly. "She thinks she killed you. The guilt has been eating at her."

"But she also thinks you betrayed her," I add, and watch that land. "In her mind, Seth—the person she trusted—turned on all of us. Worked for her abuser. Held her while Phil threatened her in front of the entire sanctuary."

Seth's breathing goes shallow. "She thinks I'm—" He can't finish.

"A traitor," Stellan supplies. "Yes."

Seth's face goes even paler, and something shifts in his expression—horror mixing with understanding.

"When I found her," he says slowly, voice rough, "her eyes opened for just a second. She looked right at me and said—" He swallows hard. "'No. It can't be him. I killed him.'"

The words land like stones in still water.

"She thought you were your mirror," I say quietly. "Coming back to finish what he started."

"And I didn't understand." Seth's hands shake. "I thought she was delirious, trapped in some nightmare. But she wasn't seeing a stranger in the dark." His voice cracks. "She was seeing the face of someone who betrayed her. Someone she thinks she murdered."

Seth's breathing turns ragged, and for a moment I think he's going to lose it completely.

"And she bonded with you anyway," Stellan says quietly.

The statement lands like a bomb.

Rhett's fire flares under his skin. "What?"

"That's not possible," Wes breathes.

Jace goes completely still. Theo's eyes unfocus for a second, then snap back with dawning understanding.

I just stare, trying to process what that means—for Bree, for all of us.

Seth looks up, confusion breaking through the grief. "I didn't—I don't even know what that means—"

"You said something locked into place when your fingers touched," Thane says, voice flat. "That was a bond forming. Her Ether claimed you."

"Even thinking he was the person who betrayed her," Stellan adds. "Her magic still reached out. That's not random. That's recognition at a level deeper than conscious thought."

"Bonds don't work like that," Wes says desperately. "They require trust—"

"They require truth," Stellan corrects. "And her magic knew the truth even when she couldn't see it."

The weight of that crashes over all of us.

Seth's voice breaks the silence, raw with guilt. "I'm sorry. I didn't try to bring her. To get her out of that chamber. Away from him."

"Away from who?" Thane's voice goes deadly quiet.

"What chamber?" Rhett demands.

Seth looks between them, exhausted and confused by their intensity. "The black stone chamber. Silver fire. He was—feeding on her, I think. She was so weak—"

"His name." Thane's voice is barely controlled. "What's his name?"

"Ethos."

The name detonates.

Wes goes pale. Rhett's fire flares hot enough to make the air shimmer. Jace curses under his breath, sharp and vicious.

But Thane—

Thane goes completely still. Then his hands start shaking.

"No." The word comes out strangled. "No, he can't—"

"You know him," Seth says, not a question.

"I was there." Thane's voice cracks. "In the Void with her. The first time. He threw us back out like we were nothing." His silver eyes are wild now, unfocused. "And now he has her. He's had her this whole time and we didn't—"

His hands curl into fists so tight I hear his knuckles crack.

"You should know," Theo says quietly, and everyone turns. "After you and Bree came back from the Void that first time, I searched. Found fragments in old scrolls." His voice is grim. "Ethos doesn't just feed. He consumes. Breaks people down until there's nothing left but what he wants them to be."

Thane's face drains of color. "And he has her."

The room goes silent.

"How bad?" He looks at Seth, and there's something desperate in Thane's expression now. "How bad is she?"

Seth's throat works. "Fading. She had new scars from the Void, and he was—" He stops, swallows hard. "She was terrified of me. But she bonded me anyway."

"Which means the bond is our anchor," Thane says, and his voice steadies with purpose. Cold calculation replacing panic. "The connection is real, stable. We can use it to navigate."

I step forward before anyone can spiral. "Then we need a plan."

"How?" Rhett demands. "How do we even get to her?"

"The bond," Wes says suddenly. "Seth said he found her. That means he got close enough to—"

"Touch her," Seth confirms.

The snake coiled around his wrist glows faintly silver, moving with its own life.

"What is that?" Wes breathes.

The door at the top of the stairs opens, and Zira appears, carrying a bundle of clothes. She descends quickly, eyes locking on Seth's wrist.

"A familiar," she says. She looks at Seth, then at the others. "Bree might not even know she has them. That one wouldn't have gone with him unless it trusted him. Unless it knew he belonged with her."

"So the bond is real," Stellan says quietly.

Zira nods. "The familiar proves it. They can feel connections we can't see."

The jealousy that flickers across Rhett's and Jace's faces is immediate. They don't say anything, but I see it—the territorial anger at someone else being bonded to her while they're stuck here, helpless.

"That's our anchor," Thane says, silver eyes fixed on Seth's wrist. "The bond connects you to her—which means it connects us to her."

"You're suggesting we use Seth to navigate," Stellan says, and there's warning in his voice.

"It's the only way," Thane says. "The Void has no landmarks, no direction. But the bond is a tether. If Seth can feel it strongly enough, we follow him."

"Through the mirrors," Theo adds quietly. "The Oath chamber responded to Bree weeks ago. The connection might still be open."

"And if it's not?" Stellan asks.

"Then we're trapped too," I say. "But at least we'll be with her."

"There's one more thing we need to talk about," Thane says. "The Oath."

Stellan nods. "If we're going into the Void—really going in, not just getting thrown back out—we need every advantage we can get."

"The Oath binds you to your mirror self," Thane continues. "Gives you access to power you wouldn't have otherwise. In the Void, that could be the difference between surviving and being consumed."

"We've been working with the Feeders who came to the sanctuary," Stellan adds. "Helping them take the Oath. Bree's Ether opened the chamber—it works now."

Wes straightens. "How many have taken it?"

"One hundred and twelve so far," Zira says, holding out the clothes to Seth. "All successful. And you look like you could use something that fits—borrowed these from Wes."

Seth takes them gratefully. "Thank you."

I look at her, then back at Thane. "You haven't taken it yet."

"No." Thane's silver eyes are steady. "We've been preparing others first. Making sure the chamber was stable."

"But now it's our turn," Stellan says.

The weight of that settles over the room.

"So we take the Oath," Jace says. "All of us. Then we go after her."

"Together," Rhett adds, and there's no question in his voice. Just certainty.

Wes nods. Theo's eyes are already distant, seeing something the rest of us can't. When he focuses again, he just says, "Yes."

"What about me?" Seth's voice is rough. "My mirror's gone. I don't know what happens if I try."

"Then we find out," I say. "If you're willing."

Seth looks down at the snake coiled around his wrist, glowing faintly silver. "She bonded me even when she thought I was the one who betrayed her. Even when she was terrified." He meets my eyes. "I'm willing."

Thane's expression shifts—something that might be approval. "Then we do this together. All of us. In an hour."

"And after?" Jace asks.

"After the Oath, Seth leads us through," Stellan says. "You opened the passage once already," he adds, looking at Seth. "Through Bree's mirror. You can do it again."

Seth nods slowly. "I can try."

"That's our way in," Thane confirms. "The bond connects you to her. You follow that connection back through the mirrors, and we follow you."

"And if Riley wakes up?" Jace's voice goes hard.

"We keep pretending," Thane says coldly. "Let her think nothing's changed. Let her believe we're still fooled."

"We have an hour to pack, gather supplies" I finish. "Then, we get Bree back."

Zira looks around the room, something flickers in her eyes. "Good. It's about time."

I watch Seth pull on the borrowed shirt—Wes's shirt—and something about that small act of normalcy steadies me. We're still here. Still functioning. Still planning.

Still fighting for her.

Rhett turns away from the group, heading toward the stairs. Jace follows without a word. I know where they're going—somewhere they can process this while gathering supplies without breaking in front of everyone else.

Theo sinks onto the floor, head in his hands.

That leaves me, Wes, Thane, Stellan, Zira, and Seth in the aftermath.

"We've got this." Thane says, and it sounds like a promise. "Let's move."

I move toward the stairs, needing air, needing space to think. As I pass the largest mirror, I catch my reflection—and for just a second, I swear I see something else.

A flicker of silver mist where there should be none.

Wrong.

I stop, staring harder, but it's gone. Just my own face looking back, tired and trying to hold it together.

But the feeling doesn't fade. That crawling sensation at the base of my skull that says something's watching.

"Gray?" Wes's voice pulls me back.

"I'm fine." I turn away from the mirror. "Just need to clear my head."

"Want company?"

I look at him—at the fear barely contained beneath his calm exterior, at the way his hands shake when he thinks no one's watching. He needs grounding as much as I need air.

"Yeah," I say. "Come on."

We head up the stairs together, leaving the others to finish planning. As we step into the night, and make our way back to the Sanctuary, I look at the place that's become home.

At the window where Bree's room is.

Where Riley sleeps in her bed, wears her face, lives her life.

And I make a silent promise.

We're coming for you, Bree.

Just hold on a little longer.

Chapter 33
THEO

The chamber hums beneath my skin like a living thing.

I stand at the center of the ritual space, surrounded by mirrors that gleam with impossible light—silver runes carved into their frames pulsing in rhythm with my heartbeat. Every surface reflects not just what I am, but what I could become—whole, complete, terrifying.

My magic vibrates through my bones, electric and urgent. Visions flicker at the edges of my perception—fractured images that won't stay still long enough to make sense.

Light. Fire. Mirrors cracking. Bree's crown gleaming silver-white.

Then—darker flashes: *black Ether curling like ink through water, a woman with Bree's face but sharper edges, silver chains wrapped around wrists I recognize.*

I blink hard, forcing the images back. Not now. I need to stay present.

But the visions keep bleeding through, insistent. Like my magic knows something I don't and is trying desperately to warn me.

"You okay?" Gray's voice cuts through the static in my head.

I turn to find him watching me with that careful intensity he reserves for moments when things might go wrong. The others are gathered around the chamber's perimeter—Rhett near the entrance, flames dancing beneath his skin; Jace perched on a broken pillar, spinning a blade between his fingers; Wes hovering close to Seth, whose familiar coils tight around his wrist.

Thane and Stellan stand at opposite ends of the mirror circle, silver and shadow in perfect balance. Zira leans against the far wall, arms crossed, expression unreadable.

"Yeah," I lie. "Just... a lot of energy in here."

Gray doesn't look convinced, but he doesn't push. That's one of the things I've always loved about him—he knows when to give space.

Thane's voice cuts through the chamber's hum. "Everyone ready?"

My gut screams that something's wrong. That we're missing something critical.

But we're out of time. Bree's trapped in the Void, and every second we waste is another second she's alone with whatever darkness lives there.

Ethos.

The name whispers through my mind, and I shudder. I've seen him in fragments—glimpses of calm, predatory patience that makes my skin crawl. He's waiting for us. Waiting for this exact moment.

But the visions won't clarify. They show me *after*—the consequences, the shattered pieces—but never *how* or *why*.

"On three," Thane says, his silver eyes scanning each of us in turn. "Everyone approaches their mirror together. Place your palm to the glass. Don't look away."

Stellan adds, "The mirror will show you your other self. Don't flinch. Don't pull back. The Oath requires recognition."

My heart pounds as I step toward the mirror directly in front of me. The glass shimmers, and for a moment, I see myself reflected—but not quite right. The eyes are the same deep brown, but there's something else in them. Certainty. Clarity. Like this version of me has never doubted a single vision.

Around me, the others move into position. Rhett's reflection flickers with heat, fire runes mirrored back at him. Jace's mirror swirls with invisible currents, air magic coiling like living wings. Gray's shows a shimmer of silver fur beneath his skin—wolf, waiting to emerge.

Wes's reflection makes him look... more. Like every perfect angle has been refined, every imperfection erased. His mirror-self is beautiful in a way that feels dangerous.

And Thane and Stellan—their reflections are darker, sharper, like they've always known exactly who they are and never apologized for it.

"Three," Thane says.

My hand lifts toward the glass.

"Two."

The chamber's hum grows louder, vibrating through my chest.

"One."

We press our palms to the mirrors.

The glass warms beneath my touch—then *glows*. Heat floods up my arm, through my chest, into my skull. I gasp, vision whiting out as power slams into me like a tidal wave.

And suddenly, I'm not alone in my head.

Voices overlap—*Rhett's fury, Jace's joy, Gray's vow, Wes's hunger, Thane's restraint*—all of them bleeding together until I can't tell where one ends and another begins. Their magic threads through mine, knotting together into something vast and terrifying and *whole*.

The mirrors flash, each projecting a sigil into the air above us. The symbols spin, merging into a single glyph that hangs suspended in the center of the chamber.

The Ashen Oath.

Light explodes through me—ecstatic, agonizing, endless. My Seer magic *burns*, carving new pathways through my mind until I feel like I'm on fire. My eyes blaze silver, tears of light streaming down my face.

I see *everything*.

Bree's crown flaring white-gold. The Council's banners burning. Phil smiling in the shadows. And beneath it all—*Ethos's eyes opening in the dark.*

The visions fracture, splitting into a thousand futures that all lead to the same place: *ruin.*

Then, just as suddenly, it stops.

I stumble backward, gasping, my hand falling away from the mirror. Around me, the others stagger too—Rhett catching himself against the wall, Jace doubling over with a sharp laugh, Gray steady but shaken.

Wes looks dazed, like he's not sure what just happened. Thane and Stellan are the only ones still standing straight, but even they look rattled.

The mirrors are no longer reflections. They're *windows*—showing other places, other versions of ourselves, other possibilities.

"Holy shit," Jace breathes.

"That was…" Wes trails off, shaking his head.

Rhett just stares at his hands, where faint fire runes now glow beneath his skin. "Did it work?"

"It worked," Stellan says, his voice tight. "You're bonded to your mirror selves now. Stronger than you were before."

Thane turns to Seth, who's been standing off to the side, watching with wide eyes. "Your turn."

Seth swallows hard, his gaze darting to the central mirror—the one directly in front of Bree's throne. "What if... what if it doesn't work?"

"Then we find out," I say, though my gut twists with unease.

Seth steps forward slowly, the familiar on his wrist glowing brighter with each step. When he reaches the mirror, he hesitates—then presses his palm to the glass.

For a moment, nothing happens.

Then the glass *ripples*.

Silver light explodes outward, so bright I have to shield my eyes. The other mirrors ignite in response, their light converging on Seth like he's the anchor holding them all together.

And then I see her.

Bree.

She's on the other side of the mirror, pale and wide-eyed, reaching toward us with trembling hands. Her lips move, but I can't hear what she's saying.

"She's there!" I gasp. "She's right there!"

Chapter 34
RHETT

The moment Seth's hand touches the mirror, everything changes.

Silver light explodes outward, so bright I have to shield my eyes. The chamber floods with warmth—not heat, but *presence*. Like standing near someone you love, close enough to feel their heartbeat through the air between you.

And then I see her.

Bree.

She's on the other side of the glass, pale and barefoot, reaching toward us with trembling hands. Her hair falls loose around her shoulders, and her eyes—those light green eyes with gold flecks—lock onto mine.

The breath leaves my lungs.

Fire knows fire. I'd know her energy anywhere—the way it calls to mine, the way my magic recognizes hers like coming home. That pull in my chest, the one I didn't even know was missing, suddenly *sings*.

Like something lost has finally been found.

The air between us hums, recognition older than memory.

Around me, the others react. Gray goes perfectly still, wolf-sharp focus locked on the mirror. Jace whispers something that might be a curse or a prayer. Wes takes a step forward, hands reaching instinctively.

But I can't look away from her face.

She's moving her lips, trying to tell us something. I lean closer, pressing my palm to the warm glass, desperate to hear—

Then I feel it.

A flicker. Just for a second. Like watching someone's reflection in water when the surface ripples.

Her chest doesn't rise and fall in rhythm with mine.

My fire reacts before my brain catches up—protective fury slamming through my veins. I conjure a small flame between my fingers without thinking, holding it up to illuminate the glass.

Through the light, I see it clearly.

The distortion. The shimmer of something *wrong*.

Her eyes are too empty. Her edges blur slightly, like she's not quite solid. And when I focus on the space around her, I can see the seams—the way reality bends to hold her shape.

Not her. An illusion. A trap.

"No," Seth gasps from beside me. He's on his knees now, staring at the mirror with devastation carved into every line of his face. "It's not her. It's *not her*."

The chamber trembles. Every mirror rattles in its frame, glass singing with stress.

My flame flares hotter in my hand, begging to be unleashed. To burn this lie away. To tear through the Void until I find the real Bree and drag her back myself.

But I force it down. Bank the heat. Breathe through the rage.

Control through love, not destruction.

"Theo?" I say, voice rough. "What do you see?"

He's clutching Stellan's arm for support, silver tears still streaming down his face. "A test," he whispers. "The Void is testing him. Testing all of us."

The illusion of Bree begins to fade, her form dissolving like smoke. Seth makes a broken sound, reaching for her even as she disappears.

Then—silence.

The mirrors go dark. The warmth vanishes. We're left standing in the chamber with nothing but our ragged breathing and the terrible weight of knowing she's still out there. Still trapped.

Seth's familiar coils tight around his wrist, pulsing with anxious light.

"I have to go," he says quietly. "The bond—it's pulling me. She's through there somewhere. I can *feel* it."

"Then we go with you," I say, stepping forward to grip his shoulder.

He looks up at me, eyes wide. "You don't have to—"

"You're one of us now," I cut him off. "We go where you go."

Gray moves to Seth's other side, steady and certain. "All of us."

Jace nods, spinning a blade between his fingers. "Not letting you have all the fun."

Wes's voice is quiet but absolute: "Together."

Theo just reaches out, touching Seth's arm. The gesture says everything.

Thane steps forward, silver eyes locked on Seth. "The bond you carry leads to her. We follow that thread."

Stellan adds from beside him, "You're not walking into the dark alone."

Zira watches from the edge of the chamber, arms crossed. "This is what the Oath meant. Shared risk. Shared blood." She meets my eyes. "Bring her home."

Seth stares at each of us in turn, something breaking and reforming in his expression. He swallows hard, then pushes to his feet.

"Okay," he whispers. "Okay."

He faces the central mirror—the one that showed us the illusion. It's dark now, just polished glass reflecting our faces back at us.

But when Seth lifts his hand toward it, the surface ripples.

His familiar slides off his wrist, transforming into pure light that snakes across the glass. The runes carved into the frame ignite one by one, silver fire racing along stone.

And the mirror *opens*.

Not shattering. Not melting. Just... opening. Like a doorway that was always there, waiting for permission.

Beyond it, I see silver mist and drifting ash. Darkness that feels alive. And somewhere in that void, a faint thread of warmth that might be her.

Seth takes a breath, steadies himself, and steps through.

The glass swallows him whole.

For a moment, nothing happens. Then every mirror in the chamber flares at once, their light converging on the central portal. The Oath sigil reappears above us—half bright, half black, spinning slowly.

I feel the burn in my chest. An invisible tether stretching between us and Seth, between us and wherever Bree is. Between us and the Void itself.

"He made his choice," I say, turning to face the others. "Now we make ours."

Gray's eyes catch the light—just for a second, they flash silver like his animal's. Wes's pupils are blown wide, the air around him humming with barely contained hunger. Jace's grin looks too sharp, too eager. Theo mutters fragments of vision under his breath, words I can't quite catch.

And Stellan—his voice drops lower, resonant with something ancient when he speaks: "Together. Or not at all."

We join hands. Fire, air, shadow, light, hunger, vision. The circuit closes, and power surges through us—volatile, amplified, barely controlled.

My fire wants to *burn*. To consume everything in its path until I find her.

But I hold it steady. Channel it into purpose instead of rage.

"Three," I say.

Heat builds beneath my skin.

"Two."

The Ether hums, answering.

"One."

We step into the light.

The world dissolves.

Heat, mist, silence.

For a moment, I'm nowhere—suspended in silver nothing, feeling the bonds between us stretch and strain but hold.

Then my feet hit solid ground.

I open my eyes to ash drifting through silver air. The sky above us isn't sky—it's void, endless and hungry. The ground beneath us is smooth black stone that reflects nothing.

The others materialize around me, one by one. Gray stumbles, catching himself. Jace lands in a crouch, blade already drawn. Wes presses a hand to his chest like he can't breathe. Theo sways, Stellan catching his arm to steady him.

Thane appears last, silver eyes scanning the landscape with predatory focus. "We're scattered," he says quietly. "Seth's bond pulled him through first. We followed, but the Void doesn't play fair with arrivals."

"Where's Seth?" Jace asks.

I turn in a slow circle, searching. But there's nothing. No landmarks. No direction. Just endless drifting embers and ashen light.

Then I hear it.

A laugh. Faint and distant, carried on wind that doesn't exist.

Bree's laugh.

My heart leaps—

Then it cuts off into a scream.

The sound is swallowed by distance before I can locate it, leaving only terrible silence.

"Bree!" I shout, fire igniting in my palms.

But the Void doesn't answer.

I force myself to breathe. To think. To remember why we're here.

Hold on, little flame, I think, sending the words out into the dark like a prayer. *We're coming.*

Around me, the others gather close. We're here. We made it through.

But as I stare into the endless black, feeling the weight of the Void pressing in from all sides, I realize the truth:

We didn't rescue her.

We walked into the trap.

And somewhere in the dark, something smiles.

The Void has us now.

THANK YOU

To My Readers

You are the light that guides this story through its darkest moments. Thank you for following Bree deeper into the mirrors—for holding space for her struggles with power and identity, and for trusting me with your hearts as everything gets more complicated.

Your messages about how these characters have become real to you, how their bonds give you hope for your own relationships—that's the magic that keeps me writing through the hardest scenes.

Thank you for staying with Bree as she learns that healing isn't linear, that sometimes you have to break before you can rebuild, and that the people who truly love you will wait while you figure out who you're becoming.

Thank you for loving Thane even when he makes terrible choices—for believing in bonds that transcend understanding, and for recognizing that sometimes the greatest act of love is stepping back when someone needs space to grow.

To anyone who has ever questioned their own reflection: Bree's journey through the mirrors is for you. You are not defined by your worst moments or your deepest fears. The parts of yourself you're afraid to face don't make you unworthy—they make you human.

To everyone who knows that sometimes love means making impossible choices—this one's for you.

And to anyone learning that power without wisdom is dangerous, but wisdom without courage is useless—Bree sees you.

Here's to facing the hard truths, choosing authenticity over perfection, and discovering that sometimes the most powerful magic is learning to love all the pieces of yourself—even the broken ones.

Sneak Peek: Shattering the Void

THANE

There's nothing here.

No sky. No ground. No horizon where one should end and the other begin.

Just black.

And we've been walking through it for what feels like a year.

The others move ahead of me in the darkness, barely visible even with my vampire sight. Rhett's dim blue flame flickers at the center of our formation—the only light we have, burning on nothing but his stubborn refusal to let it die.

Rhett insists it's fire. Personally, I think it's just his temper.

It's not enough to see by. Barely enough to convince me we still exist.

I stopped counting days somewhere around three hundred scratches on the obsidian shard I carry in my pocket. Time doesn't work here anyway—days stretch into weeks, hours collapse into seconds. But my body knows. The way my hands shake when I try to summon power I no longer have. The fact that I can't remember what her voice sounds like anymore.

That's the worst part.

Not the hunger, not the cold, not even the certainty that we might never escape.

It's that I'm forgetting her.

The exact cadence of her breath when she slept. The way her Ether curled when she was afraid but trying to hide it. The softness in her eyes right before she let herself trust me—really trust me.

It's slipping away, piece by piece, and I can't stop it.

We've tried everything.

Spells drawn in blood that Theo picked up somewhere. Rift-tears forced open with raw power we couldn't afford to spend. Bargains whispered to things that live in the spaces between breaths. Every door we make, the Void eats. Every escape route closes before we can follow it through.

Even Stellan's calm has cracked—which I didn't think was possible. Apparently the Void has stronger opinions than I do.

I caught him three turns of Rhett's fire ago — what passes for night here — whispering to something in the dark. Bartering bits of his soul like spare change in exchange for a way out.

"Please tell him I need him," he'd said, voice raw in a way I've never heard from him before.

I didn't interrupt. Desperation makes equals of us all.

And I don't know who the fuck he was talking to. Maybe he's as lost as I am.

Gray crouches ahead in his dire wolf form, motionless except for the subtle shift of his shoulders. Hunting. He insisted before his shift that he could find her this way—track her through instinct where logic failed us. That was months ago. Now he either can't shift back or won't. I'm not sure which possibility is worse.

Wes sits behind Gray, thinner than he should be. We all are, but it shows on him worst—hunger etched into every line of his face. He feeds on memory now, on ghost-impressions of emotion that cling to the things we carry.

If you catch him staring too long at someone, check your nostalgia—he might be sipping it.

It's not enough. It's never enough.

Jace talks to the echoes because silence is worse. His voice drifts over from the far edge of our makeshift camp, one-sided conversation with things that sometimes answer and sometimes don't. I don't stop him. Madness is just another tool for survival here. Sometimes the echoes answer. Honestly, they're better company than most of us.

Theo sleeps.

He always sleeps too much or not at all. When he's awake, his eyes are unfocused, seeing things the rest of us can't. When he's asleep, he dreams the same thing every time.

Bree's face, turning away.

Stellan sits beside Rhett's fire, statue-still. He conserves everything now—words, movement, even breath. The only time he stirs is when Wes starts to fade too far, and then Stellan moves with eerie precision, offering just enough of himself to keep Wes from unraveling completely.

I don't ask what it costs him.

I already know.

We walk toward the faint pull in the dark, following the only thing that ever changes—small shifts in pressure, variations in the oppressive weight of nothing. They might mean we're still inside time. They might mean nothing at all.

But it's all we have.

Every once in a while the air shifts and I swear I smell her—vanilla, ozone, heartbreak—but it's just the Void mocking me.

The ground trembles.

Subtle at first—barely perceptible. But I feel it through the soles of my boots, and my head snaps up. The darkness around us shivers, the oppressive black bleeding silver, like ink remembering how to be light.

Then a sound breaks the silence.

Sharp. Ragged. Too loud.

Theo.

I'm moving before I've finished the thought, crossing the camp in three strides. He's sitting up, chest heaving, eyes wide and wild in the dim firelight.

"What did you see?" My voice comes out harsher than I intend, but I don't soften it.

Theo's gaze locks on mine, and for the first time in months, there's something other than despair in his expression.

Hope.

Fragile and desperate, but real.

"She's alive," he gasps.

The words hit me and I can't catch my breath. I feel the others stirring, moving closer. Rhett's fire flares brighter. Gray abandons his hunt and turns toward us. Even Stellan lifts his head.

"Bree?" Wes's voice cracks on her name.

Theo nods, frantic. "I saw her. Not—not like before. Not a memory. A *vision*." He presses his palms against his temples, breathing hard. "She's chained. Surrounded by mirrors. But she's breathing. The air around her moves again."

"Where?" Rhett demands.

"I don't—" Theo shakes his head. "Deep. Deeper than we've gone. But she's *here*, in the Void. We can reach her."

For a moment, no one speaks.

The ground trembles again, stronger this time. The silver threads through the darkness multiply, spreading like cracks in ice.

The Void is reacting.

Because she is.

"Move." My voice cuts through the shock, sharp and decisive. "Gather everything. We leave now."

"Thane—" Jace starts.

"*Now.*"

They scatter, trained by months of survival to obey without question when my tone leaves no room for argument. Weapons pulled from makeshift sheaths—mirror-glass daggers, chains forged from scar-metal, anything that can hold an edge in this place.

Rhett extinguishes the fire with a flick of his wrist, plunging us into darkness relieved only by the faint silver glow threading through the Void.

I turn to Theo. "Can you track it?"

He nods, already moving. "This way. I can feel her now—like a pull."

Gray falls into step beside him, senses sharpened. Wes follows close behind, steadier than he's been in weeks. Jace and Rhett flank the group, weapons ready. Stellan brings up the rear, silent but present.

And I take point.

Because if there's a door, I'll kick it open. If there's a wall, I'll tear it down. If something stands between us and her, I'll rip it apart with my bare hands.

The Void shifts around us as we move, shadows curling and retreating. We're not the same men who fell into this place a year ago.

We're something harder now. Sharper.

Desperate enough to burn the world if it means bringing her home.

The silver light grows stronger ahead, and for the first time in months, I let myself believe.

If the world's still out there when we break through, we'll fight our way back to it

If it isn't, then we'll make one.

Continue with Bree on her journey in Shattering the Void.

ABOUT THE AUTHOR

Zora Stone writes romantasy with teeth: fierce heroines, protective men who'd burn the world for them, and enough emotional wreckage to keep things interesting. When she's not plotting betrayals or steamy chaos, she's drinking iced coffee, dodging laundry, or daydreaming about enchanted forests.

You can find her online at:

Website: ZoraStone.com

TikTok | Instagram: @ZoraStoneAuthor

And on Amazon and Goodreads.

Want behind-the-scenes chaos and sneak peeks? ZoraStone.com/Influencers

ALSO BY ZORA STONE

The Ether Chronicles

Crown of the Mist
Into the Ether
Ashen Oath
Veil of Echoes
Shattering the Void
To the Final End

Arcanum Academy

Shadows of Change
Shadows Rising
Shadows Found
Shadows Revealed